# Charlie & Frog

a
mystery

## KAREN KANE

Text copyright © 2018 by Karen Kane
Interior illustrations copyright © by 2018 Carlisle Robinson

First Hardcover Edition, April 2018
First Paperback Edition, March 2019
 3 5 7 9 10 8 6 4 2
FAC-025438-19193
Printed in the United States of America

This book is set in Adobe Caslon/Monotype
Designed by Marci Senders

Library of Congress Cataloging-in-Publication Control Number for Hardcover Edition: 2017032004
ISBN 978-1-368-00630-9

Visit www.DisneyBooks.com

To David, Hayley, and Isa
and to my mom, Louise
to my dad, Billy
and to my grandma Vera,
who taught me Kings Corners

# 1. Criminal

Charlie's grandparents forgot he was in the room, which is how he ended up watching *Vince Vinelli's Worst Criminals Ever!*, wrapped in a blanket, terrified yet unable to look away. Charlie wished someone would send him to bed, but his parents had yet to come home from their date night and his grandparents had yet to turn around in their E-Z chair recliners and notice him. Also his grandparents couldn't hear very well, so the criminals and their crimes were at full volume.

"When crime is a fact, good people act!" Vince Vinelli pointed his finger right at Charlie. "Good people do good things!"

"Good people—that means us, Irving!" Grandma Tickler shouted at Grandpa Tickler. "It's a good thing good people like us watch this show—a criminal could be anywhere."

"Ayuh," Grandpa Tickler said.

Charlie fingerspelled the word "criminal" with his left hand.

CRIMINAL.

At the end of the show, Vince Vinelli asked viewers to call a toll-free number if they spotted a criminal featured on the program. Grandma Tickler kept the telephone next to her recliner, ready to call, but of course she never did. Grandma and Grandpa Tickler never went anywhere except to the doctor's office.

Grandma and Grandpa Tickler were, to put it bluntly, lousy grandparents. They would never think to take Charlie to the zoo or play a game with him or turn around to tell him to go to bed because a TV show was too scary for him to watch.

But if Charlie's grandparents hadn't been so lousy, Charlie might never have met Frog.

He might never have learned sign language.

He might never have solved a murder mystery.

## 2. Giant Golden Moles

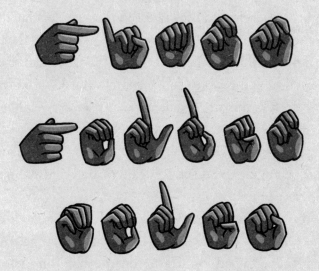

Charlie's grandparents weren't the only lousy ones. Charlie's parents were lousy, too.

They never tucked Charlie in at night or made sure he ate his broccoli. They never bought Charlie new socks when his old ones were too holey to wear. They never remembered that Charlie's toothbrush needed to be replaced every three months as suggested by the American Dental Association.

No, Charlie had to do all those things for himself. But Charlie's parents weren't all bad—they liked to help. In particular they liked to help animals.

They helped yellow-blotched turtles in Mississippi,

lesser long-nosed bats in New Mexico, and piping plovers in Montana. They traveled to Cozumel Island to help pygmy raccoons, and they traipsed through Australia to locate northern hairy-nosed wombats—and help them.

This would have been exciting if Charlie had been allowed to come along and help, too. But Charlie was always left in the care of a nanny who was near—but not too near—wherever his parents were helping. Eventually Mr. and Mrs. Tickler would return, pack up Charlie and their belongings, and set off again to find new animals that needed help.

But this time Charlie's parents had a better idea. This time they had packed up Charlie and their belongings and stopped by Castle-on-the-Hudson before flying off to—

"Africa," Mr. Tickler said the next morning.

Grandpa Tickler cupped a hand to his ear.

"They want to leave Charlie with us," Grandma Tickler shouted to Grandpa Tickler, "because moles in Africa need them!"

"Giant golden moles," Mr. Tickler said, "in South Africa, to be precise."

"So that's why you're here," Grandma Tickler said. "We wondered why you came to visit us. With so many suitcases, too. You haven't visited us once since Charlie was little, you know."

Charlie sat on the top of the stairs. He eavesdropped

4

and fingerspelled GIANT GOLDEN MOLES. Yvette, his grandparents' housekeeper, was vacuuming the upstairs hallway—with the vacuum turned off. She could see Charlie was eavesdropping and glared at him. But Yvette was eavesdropping, too, so Charlie ignored her and concentrated on the conversation in the parlor.

"We're terribly sorry we haven't visited more often," Mrs. Tickler said. "But we've been busy, you see, busy with important work."

"So busy," Mr. Tickler said, "that we forgot about the two of you. And when we did remember, we remembered you are grandparents, and grandparents can be very useful."

"Exactly," Mrs. Tickler said. "Why have a nanny when there are grandparents available?"

"Well . . ." Grandma Tickler began.

Charlie leaned forward.

"It's not that we don't want Charlie here, but we have very busy lives. Every morning we eat breakfast and take our pills. Then we have a doctor's appointment— sometimes two appointments, isn't that right, Irving?"

"Ayuh," Grandpa Tickler said.

"Then we eat lunch," Grandma Tickler went on, "then nap, then dinner, then our shows. We have our game shows, our cooking shows . . ."

"Don't know why they watch cooking shows," Yvette whispered. "I do all the cooking."

". . . our news shows. There are horrible things we need to know about. Then we have our investigative crime shows."

"Ayuh," Grandpa Tickler agreed.

"Charlie is very independent," Mr. Tickler said.

"And," Mrs. Tickler added, "he doesn't need much care."

Charlie leaned back and rested his chin in his hands.

"I suppose we could keep him," Grandma Tickler said, "if Charlie doesn't need us to do anything. And I suppose if he does need something, like help with bathing and such, Yvette could do it."

Yvette shook her head and swiped her duster like a sword. She glared even harder at Charlie, who, at ten years old, was insulted his grandparents thought he needed help bathing.

And so it had been decided. Charlie's parents were to leave for South Africa to help giant golden moles, while Charlie was to be left in an enormous house with two old people and their housekeeper, none of whom wanted him there.

# 3. Stay

Mr. Tickler held up his Speedo and fingerspelled BATHING SUIT. "Should I bring one bathing suit or two?" he asked Mrs. Tickler.

As a boy, Mr. Tickler had learned some American Sign Language. Although he had forgotten most of the signs, he remembered the manual alphabet. He taught Mrs. Tickler how to fingerspell so they could communicate in the wilderness and not make a sound. They practiced constantly.

"Bring two," Mrs. Tickler advised. "That way one bathing suit can completely dry. Putting on a wet bathing suit is a terrible thing."

Charlie's fingers flew as his parents sorted through their belongings, deciding what to pack for South Africa. TERRIBLE THING. Charlie learned to fingerspell by watching his parents. He was much faster than either one of them.

"You can't pack a big bottle of sunscreen in your carry-on suitcase," Charlie reminded his mother. BOTTLE.

"Oh, you're right, darling. Thanks," Mrs. Tickler said and fingerspelled:

T. Pause.

H. Pause.

A. Pause.

N. Pause.

K. Pause.

S!

Mrs. Tickler gave a satisfied sigh and went back to her packing.

"Castle-on-the-Hudson is a marvelous village, Charlie," Mr. Tickler said. "You can explore on your own, just like I did as a kid. I'll leave you some spending money. I wonder if Mr. Woo still works at the library."

Mr. Tickler reached into his pocket and pulled out some bills. "Gee, I only have hundred-dollar bills. You don't happen to have any change, do you, Charlie?"

Mrs. Tickler snapped her suitcase shut. "Now, darling, we will only be gone for three weeks."

"Really?" Charlie asked. Last time his parents were gone for three months.

"Of course! After all, we have to take you to that faraway boarding school on September first."

"Boarding school? What boarding school?"

"The boarding school we enrolled you in," Mrs. Tickler said, "far away from us. I thought we told you. Didn't we tell Charlie, Alistair?"

"I thought we had," Mr. Tickler said. "Now, Charlie, about that change?"

"You didn't tell me," Charlie said. "You never said anything about sending me to boarding school. I don't want to go to boarding school."

Actually Charlie didn't know what he wanted except that he wanted to be *asked* what he wanted.

"Of course you want to go," Mrs. Tickler said. "And more importantly, we want you to go. It's getting far too complicated to find care for you while we do our helping."

"Why can't I stay here?" Charlie asked. "With Grandma and Grandpa Tickler?"

"Three weeks is one thing," Mr. Tickler said. "Forever is another. But who knows? Maybe your grandparents will want you to stay forever!"

Mr. and Mrs. Tickler burst into peals of laughter.

"Oh, that's a good one!" Mrs. Tickler said, wiping her eyes. "There you go, Charlie. Get your grandparents to want you to stay forever. You have three weeks to do it."

A horn honked outside. Mr. and Mrs. Tickler hurried to finish their packing. A wizened little man named Herman had arrived to pick them up. His taxi looked even older than he did. Mrs. Tickler handed Herman her carry-on bag. Herman struggled before he finally let it drop to the ground.

"I'll get it," Charlie said. He quickly stowed the carry-on bag into the trunk along with the rest of the luggage.

Charlie's parents had already said good-bye to Grandma and Grandpa Tickler. They started to say their good-byes to Charlie, but Herman, not realizing the Ticklers weren't in the car yet, slowly started driving away. Mr. and Mrs. Tickler jumped into the moving taxi, stuck their heads out of the window, and waved.

"Good-bye, Charlie! Good-bye, darling! Wish us luck! We'll call and write if we can!"

"Wear your seat belts!" Charlie yelled as Herman rolled out of sight.

Charlie lowered his waving hand. He wanted to run after Herman's taxi and tell his parents one thing. One very important thing.

STAY.

# 4. Dangerous

A storm blustered through Castle-on-the-Hudson the day Charlie's parents left town. Rain pounded on the roof and lashed at the windows while Charlie explored his grandparents' house. He opened doors and drawers, and investigated nooks and crannies. Everything was very dusty. Yvette cleaned with a feather duster, true. But she did so while reading a book.

Lightning lit up the living room just before dinner. The television sizzled and went blank.

"Yvette!" Grandma Tickler hollered. "Lightning hit the antenna again!"

Yvette came out of the kitchen. "I'll call Herman later," she said.

"Tell him to come now," Grandma Tickler said. "It's an emergency!"

"Herman cannot fix an antenna in a lightning storm," Yvette said.

"Why not?" Grandma Tickler demanded.

"Herman the taxi driver?" Charlie said. "He's going to fix the antenna on the roof?" Charlie couldn't imagine the little man fixing something on the ground, much less something that high up.

"Herman can fix anything," Grandma Tickler said. "We had a special harness made in case he falls off the ladder. Or the roof."

"Ayuh," Grandpa Tickler said.

"I hope we eat soon," Grandma Tickler said, "because now we have nothing else to do."

• • •

The next day the sun shone hot and bright. Herman stepped out of the taxi and strapped on the harness. Charlie stood outside and watched. Herman gripped the edges of the ladder. He placed one foot on the first step, braced himself, and then pulled the other foot up. He paused and took a breath. Charlie counted one-Mississippi, two-Mississippi, three-Mississippi.

Then Herman placed a foot on the second rung. He braced, then (one-Mississippi, two-Mississippi, three-Mississippi) pulled himself up.

Charlie went inside. Grandma and Grandpa Tickler were sitting in their E-Z chair recliners, waiting for the TV to turn on again. Charlie was anxious to see the village.

"Can I walk to the library?" he asked.

"Too dangerous," Grandma Tickler said. "Criminals are out there, waiting to pounce."

"Dad told me he used to walk to the library alone when he was my age," Charlie said as his hand finger-spelled DANGEROUS.

"Then take a weapon," Grandma Tickler advised as she stood up. "Vince Vinelli recommends a key. You'll need to know how to use it. Irving! Help me show Charlie the secret to self-defense."

Grandpa Tickler popped out of his E-Z chair recliner with surprising speed.

"Hold the key like this, Charlie." Grandma Tickler gripped the front door key tightly. "Now, Irving, try and rob me."

"Ayuh," Grandpa Tickler said.

Charlie's grandparents turned to face each other and bowed. Like two archnemeses, they slowly circled each other. Grandma Tickler threw the first punch. Grandpa tried to spin around, but toppled over instead. Charlie caught him just in time. Grandpa Tickler shrugged off the help. He ruthlessly sliced air. Finally, in slow motion, he lunged toward Grandma Tickler, who punched him in the arm with the house key. Grandpa Tickler grabbed his arm and staggered backward.

"Fire!" Grandma Tickler shouted.

Charlie jumped. "Fire? Where?"

"Vince Vinelli says if you yell 'fire,' people come running," Grandma Tickler said. "If you yell 'thief,' people ignore you."

Yvette came down the stairs with her feather duster and book. "Irma and Irving, isn't there a show you should be getting ready to watch?"

Grandma Tickler tucked the house key into Charlie's hand.

"Criminals," Grandma Tickler said as she headed back to her recliner. "They're everywhere."

# 5. Thank You

Charlie kept a watchful eye as he walked. But Castle-on-the-Hudson, with its leafy green streets and Victorian houses painted in bright colors, did not seem like a place where criminals came to commit crimes. Charlie turned onto a street crowded with cafés and shops. Outside a café called Coffee & Cookies, a dog was drinking from a water bowl.

A young couple passed by the dog.

"What do you mean there's no cell phone service?" The man held his phone up to his ear. "We're an hour north of New York City."

"There's something odd about this place," the woman said. "Cell phones don't work, and there are red telephone booths everywhere."

Charlie walked past the couple and toward a pink Victorian home on the corner of State and Main Streets. He read the crooked plaque affixed to a large stone near the sidewalk.

CASTLE-ON-THE-HUDSON

PUBLIC LIBRARY

ESTABLISHED 1899

A tiny old woman sat knitting on the library steps, craning her neck to peer down the street. She looked at Charlie, tapped her wrist, and gestured impatiently toward the library.

"It's not ten yet," Charlie said. "Five more minutes."

The woman returned to her knitting and looking.

Knit, crane, look.

Knit, crane, look.

Charlie breathed in the coffee-scented air that swirled around the village. He gazed toward the Hudson River. He noticed two cables stretching from the village riverfront to a castle perched high on a cliff. Charlie glanced back at the library. The woman patted the porch step and gestured for him to sit down.

"Oh. No, thank you," Charlie said. "I'm fine."

The tiny woman patted the porch step again—much harder this time—and pointed at Charlie. He walked up the steps and sat down. She had a red knitted flower pinned to her dress, and a large black mole on her wrinkled cheek. The mole looked bigger and bigger the longer Charlie stared at it. The woman continued knitting from a ball of red yarn.

It was awkward sitting in silence together.

"I'm Charlie," Charlie said at last.

The woman didn't respond. Instead she pointed to her wrist again with a questioning look. Why didn't she just speak?

Charlie showed her his watch. "It's only nine fifty-seven."

She touched the fingertips of her hand to her chin, and then brought her hand forward.

Sign language! She was using sign language. He bet that sign meant "thank you."

Charlie pointed to himself. CHARLIE, he fingerspelled.

The woman put down her knitting needles. Her small hands flurried with signs.

Charlie shook his head. I DON'T UNDERSTAND, he fingerspelled again.

The woman sighed. She pointed to herself and fingerspelled her name. AGGIE. Then she picked up her knitting and continued her watchful waiting.

Knit, crane, look.

Knit, crane, look.

Aggie wasn't just watching and waiting. Aggie was watching, waiting, and worrying. Aggie was on the verge of tears.

Charlie tapped her shoulder. ARE YOU OKAY? he asked.

Aggie shook her head and opened her watery eyes wide. Charlie knew that trick. It didn't always work to keep the tears from falling, though. Before Charlie could ask another question, a lady with a bun of bubble-gum-pink hair that perfectly matched the bubble-gum-pink library marched up the sidewalk. Aggie shoved her knitting into her canvas bag and stood. She was only a little taller than Charlie.

The pink-haired lady held a pitcher of iced tea with floating slices of peach. She wore a name tag—MISS TWEEDY, ACTING LIBRARIAN.

"Lovely day for knitting," Miss Tweedy said to Aggie. Then she looked down through her pointy glasses at Charlie. "Are you Charlie Tickler, Irma and Irving's grandson?"

Charlie nodded. How did she know that?

"If you are wondering how I knew that, the answer is simple," Miss Tweedy said. "You have Irving's nose." She gazed up at the library as Charlie felt his nose.

"It's time you were opened, wouldn't you agree?"

Miss Tweedy asked the library. "Well, you'll have to wait a few minutes longer." She sat down next to Charlie.

Aggie stamped her foot. Miss Tweedy looked up. Aggie tapped her wrist and pointed to the library door.

Miss Tweedy nodded. "I completely agree—punctuality is so important. However, I dropped my library keys in Herman's taxi yesterday. Herman promised to meet me here at ten and return them."

"Aggie is Deaf," Charlie said. "She uses sign language."

"Is that so? It just so happens I'm fluent in sign language!" Miss Tweedy said. "But I'm also extremely forgetful. Give me a moment—it'll come back to me."

Aggie pulled a pencil and paper from her bag. She gestured for Miss Tweedy to write. Miss Tweedy explained about waiting for the library keys. Aggie shook her head and sat back down. The open-eye trick hadn't worked. A tear slid down her cheek.

"It's awful when a patron is upset when the library doesn't open on time," Miss Tweedy said. "I wish I had glasses out here to serve peach iced tea. Everything is better with peach iced tea."

"I think it's more than that," Charlie said. "I think Aggie is worried about something."

Miss Tweedy took Aggie's pencil again and wrote: *What's wrong? Can we help you?*

Aggie rubbed the tear away with the back of her hand and wrote: *I need to get into the library—now.*

"See?" Miss Tweedy said. "It is about the library."

"Ask her *why*," Charlie said. "Why does she need to get in?"

Miss Tweedy did. Aggie read her question and gave a ragged sigh. Finally she wrote: *I did something awful. Really awful.*

"Oh dear," Miss Tweedy said. "I wasn't expecting that. Whatever could it be?"

"Ask her," Charlie said.

Miss Tweedy wrote down the question for Aggie.

*I told a secret,* Aggie replied. *I have to fix it before something happens.*

Before something happens? Miss Tweedy didn't need Charlie's urging to write: *Like what?*

*Theft!* Aggie wrote. *Or destruction! Or worse!*

"How horrendous!" Miss Tweedy said.

A car honked.

"Oh, there's Herman. Get the keys for me, would you, Charlie?"

Charlie hurried to the curb. The taxi slowed but did not stop. Herman flung the keys through the open passenger window.

Aggie's leg quivered as she waited for Miss Tweedy to unlock the door. Once the library was open, Aggie hurried in and disappeared into the library stacks.

Charlie hoped Aggie could right her wrong—whatever it was.

The inside of the library, like the outside of the library, did not look at all like a library.

It was more like a house with too many books and no place to put them. Books that did not fit onto the shelves were piled on tables and on the floor next to big, squishy chairs. A grandfather clock ticktocked in a corner. A portrait of a stern man in a pink suit hung above the fireplace.

Charlie stumbled over a cat that had wandered from between the stacks. The cat eyed Charlie with irritation.

Miss Tweedy hurried to the circulation desk, where she pulled white cards from the backs of books, dabbed a rubber stamp with ink, and stamped the cards.

*Thwack!*

"Miss Tweedy?" Charlie said.

*Thwack!*

"I'd like to—"

*Thwack!*

"Get-a-library-card-please," Charlie finished in a rush, before the next thwack.

Miss Tweedy paused her *thwack*ing long enough to peer at Charlie through her pointy glasses.

"Peach iced tea?"

"What?"

"Would you care for some peach iced tea?"

Miss Tweedy gestured to the iced tea pitcher sitting on the counter. "Enid makes the best peach iced tea. Everything is better with peach iced tea, don't you think?" Pink lipstick covered Miss Tweedy's front teeth.

"No, thank you," Charlie said. "Just a library card, please." He casually rubbed a finger over his own front teeth, hoping Miss Tweedy would get the hint. Miss Tweedy did not.

"My offer of peach iced tea was my way of stalling for time," Miss Tweedy said. Her voice dropped to a whisper. "Visitors typically aren't allowed library cards."

She bit her bottom lip with a look of tender sympathy.

"But I'm not a visitor," Charlie said. "I'm living here with my grandparents."

That was true—he did live here. At least for now.

"Oh, that makes me feel better," Miss Tweedy said. "I need an ID and a reference."

"A reference?"

"Yes, a reference. Someone who will vouch that you will take proper care of library books. I can't just be handing out books to anyone! What would Mr. Woo say?" Miss Tweedy pointed. Charlie's eyes followed the angle of her finger to the portrait of the pink-suited man hanging over the fireplace.

"I don't have a reference or an ID," Charlie said.

Miss Tweedy clucked her tongue. "We shall deal with that when I return. For now, please take over the circulation desk for me while I"—Miss Tweedy tapped her collarbone—"visit Mrs. Murphy."

"What do you mean, take over?" Charlie asked.

"If a patron comes in, show him or her how to use the Dewey decimal system. If a book is returned"—*thwack*—"stamp the card in the back. That sort of thing. Mr. Dickens will help you." Miss Tweedy went through a door behind the circulation desk and closed it firmly behind her.

"Mr. Dickens will help me? Who is Mr. Dickens?"

Charlie stood awkwardly next to the circulation desk. He hoped Miss Tweedy's visit with Mrs. Murphy, whomever Mrs. Murphy was, wouldn't take long.

Charlie heard Aggie somewhere in the library, making a low, frustrated sound. Before Charlie could go check on her, she rushed out of the library stacks. Aggie pointed toward the circulation desk and gestured with her arms wide, palms up, frantically looking for Miss Tweedy.

Charlie shrugged his shoulders and fingerspelled BACK SOON.

Aggie paced. Suddenly her eyes darted to the front windows. She stood on her tiptoes and stared outside. She spun back around, eyes wide with fright.

Aggie slung large, hard signs at Charlie.

She was desperately trying to tell Charlie something. I DON'T UNDERSTAND.

Aggie fumbled to pull the pencil from her knitting

bag. The pencil fell to the floor and rolled under a bookshelf. Aggie's hands were shaking. Charlie hurried around the circulation desk to find another pencil. Aggie signed to Charlie once more, a pleading look in her eyes. Then she threw up her hands and disappeared.

What was Aggie trying to tell him? And what had she seen through the front windows? Charlie was about to go over and look when two men walked into the library.

# 6. Wrong

The cozy library suddenly did not feel so cozy anymore.

The cat peered around a bookshelf and hissed at the two men.

"You sure you saw her, Dex?" the taller man asked the shorter man with the huge neck.

"How do I know?" said Dex with the huge neck. "I've only seen her once before—on Tony's phone."

The men noticed Charlie standing behind the circulation desk, staring at them.

"You the librarian?" Dex asked. His voice was easy, but his eyes were not.

"Um, I guess," Charlie said. "Temporarily."

"Did a little old woman come in here?" the tall man asked. "She has this thing on her cheek—"

"A mole, Ray. For the thousandth time it's called a mole."

"Yeah, a mole," Ray said. "Is she here?"

"I don't know," Charlie said.

"What do you mean, you don't know?" Ray asked.

"Forget it," Dex said. "I'll look upstairs. You look down here."

Charlie stood frozen. He couldn't yell for Aggie to run—she couldn't hear him. He could yell for Miss Tweedy and Mrs. Murphy—but why did he feel the need to yell at all? It was a public library. The two men weren't doing anything. They were just looking.

Then why was Aggie so afraid? Charlie wondered. And why was *he* so afraid, too?

Dex came back downstairs. Ray came out of the stacks.

"No one's here except the kid," Ray said. He handed Dex a stick of gum. "Where next?"

"We look everywhere." Dex opened the gum. "We find her, we find it," he continued as he gave the wrapper back to Ray.

"What exactly are we looking for?"

"Not sure." Dex opened the library door. "But we'll know it when we see it."

"Right. 'It.' Whatever 'it' is." Ray folded a stick of

gum into his mouth. He turned over his hand and opened his fist. Two gum wrappers fluttered to the floor. Ray grinned at Charlie before following Dex out the door.

When he was sure they were gone, Charlie started his own search for Aggie. Upstairs, downstairs, around shelves, under the tables—Aggie was nowhere to be found.

Charlie had searched the downstairs twice before he noticed a window open in the back. He leaned out. Aggie's knitting bag sat beneath the windowsill in a heap. How did Aggie's knitting bag get there? Did Aggie leave the library through the window? Charlie climbed out the window, hopped to the ground, and picked up the knitting bag. He walked around the library. Aggie was still nowhere to be found.

Two sugar-free cinnamon gum wrappers greeted Charlie in the library doorway. He picked them up and returned to the circulation desk.

"Did everything go well?" Miss Tweedy asked as she whipped open the door.

"No," Charlie said. "I think Aggie left the library through a window."

"We shouldn't judge patrons by how they choose to leave a library," Miss Tweedy said. "And who is Aggie?"

"Aggie. The woman who came into the library with

us. She was really upset, Miss Tweedy. Two men came looking for her—but she disappeared out the back and dropped her bag." Charlie held up the knitting bag.

"She was probably upset because a book she wanted wasn't on the shelf," Miss Tweedy said. "That always upsets me terribly."

"I don't know why she was upset," Charlie said. "She used sign language. Maybe it had something to do with her secret. Remember she said she told a secret?"

"Well, do you remember anything she signed?"

Charlie pictured what Aggie's hands were doing just before she disappeared. He showed Miss Tweedy the one thing he remembered.

Miss Tweedy shook her head. "You must be remembering wrong," Miss Tweedy said, "because I have never seen that sign before in my life. And I happen to be fluent in sign language! But here's a sign for you to learn."

Miss Tweedy signed the letter *Y*, and then touched the *Y* to her chin with her palm facing inward. "This is the sign for 'wrong.' You must be remembering wrong!" Miss Tweedy signed "wrong" several times to make sure Charlie understood how wrong he was.

"I am pretty sure what I showed you was right," Charlie said. Nonetheless, his hand practiced the sign Miss Tweedy had just shown him. "*Wrong*."

"And I am pretty sure you're wrong," Miss Tweedy

said. "However, if you insist on being disagreeable, you should consult an expert. Go into the Flying Hands Café up at the castle. Ask for my sign language teacher—Frog Castle. You can ride the gondola there. Mr. Simple is the gondola operator. It costs one dollar to ride and the schedule changes daily."

"Um, okay," Charlie said.

"Frog will help you figure out what Aggie said. And when you find Aggie, you can return her bag."

"Can you come—I mean, don't you want to come with me?" Charlie asked.

Miss Tweedy gestured around the empty library. "You can see I am extremely busy! I not only run the Castle-on-the-Hudson Library, but I also curate the Castle-on-the-Hudson Museum. What do you do?"

Good point. Charlie did not do anything.

"All right," Charlie said. He remembered Aggie's frightened eyes. He needed to make sure she was okay. Hopefully he could just walk around the village and find her.

"Now," Miss Tweedy said. "It's time to issue you a library card." She gave a happy clap of her hands. "This is my favorite part of librarian work!" Miss Tweedy lugged an old typewriter out from under the desk.

"Frog Castle," Charlie repeated. "Castle is his last name?"

"*Her* last name. Yes, it is. The Castle family is an old and venerable family. They have been in the Hudson Valley for hundreds of years. They built the castle in honor of their family name. And our village named itself Castle-on-the-Hudson in honor of them. Your name, please?"

"Charlie Tickler."

"I have a feeling," Miss Tweedy said, "that you've told me that before. I'm horrid with names. Numbers, however, I always remember. If your name had a number attached to it, then I would definitely remember it, wouldn't I, Mr. Dickens?" Miss Tweedy cooed at the cat that had jumped up onto the circulation desk. So this was Mr. Dickens. Mr. Dickens eyed Charlie with regal regard.

Miss Tweedy seemed to have forgotten about IDs and references, and typed up Charlie's library card. She insisted she had the perfect book for Charlie to read. She found it, checked it out to him, and then ushered Charlie out of the library with the book and the knitting bag stuffed in his arms.

"Remember!" Miss Tweedy called after him. "Gondola over to the castle, Flying Hands Café, ask for Frog."

Charlie stood for a moment outside the library and thought. Perhaps there was something in Aggie's knitting bag, some kind of clue. He rummaged through it to find the paper Aggie and Miss Tweedy had written on, and knitting needles stuck in a long knitted piece wrapped around a ball of red yarn.

Okay. So he would walk around the village and look for Aggie, Charlie reasoned. But what if he ran into Dex and Ray? So what? What was the big deal? They were just two men who had come into the library. Even if they had seemed scary. Even if Aggie had been frightened enough to climb out the library window. Criminals didn't come to villages like Castle-on-the-Hudson, did they?

No, they did not.

As he walked around the village, Charlie practiced fingerspelling in case he found Aggie. WHAT WERE YOU TRYING TO TELL ME?

Charlie did not find Aggie or run into Dex and Ray.

Charlie's next option was to cross the river and find Frog Castle. A gondola ride seemed like something he should ask permission from Grandma and Grandpa Tickler to do. Charlie was certain grandparents would want to know their grandson was dangling from a wire hundreds of feet above a wide, deep rushing river. They might even say they would worry if he went alone. They might even want to come along to make sure he was all right.

• • •

"Just take your key," Grandma Tickler said, after Charlie had arrived home and asked about riding the gondola. "For the criminals, you know."

"Ayuh," Grandpa Tickler said.

"The gondola crosses the river," Charlie said. "Don't you want to—"

"Hush, Charlie," Grandma Tickler said. "Our show is back on."

If no one was going to worry about Charlie, then Charlie would have to worry for himself. Was it safe to cross the river? And even if he made it across the river, what could he really do? Charlie was just a kid. Besides, Charlie tried to reassure himself, Aggie was probably fine.

For the rest of the afternoon Charlie worried and read the book Miss Tweedy had insisted he check out: *Danny, the Champion of the World* by Roald Dahl. The afternoon turned into evening. Yvette had left meat loaf in the oven for him and his grandparents. Charlie took a cautious bite. It looked like a gray brick but tasted like gravy and beef.

*Vince Vinelli's Worst Criminals Ever!* blared from the television once again. Charlie couldn't help but get pulled into the show. He wrapped himself in a blanket and watched from the sofa while Grandma and Grandpa Tickler watched from their E-Z chair recliners.

Grandpa Tickler hung on Vince Vinelli's every

word. Charlie, on the other hand, was hung up staring at Grandpa Tickler's large, bulbous nose. What was Miss Tweedy talking about? His nose wasn't anything like Grandpa Tickler's.

"What was the hardest part of your ordeal?" Vince Vinelli asked a crime victim.

"The hardest part," the woman said, "was people saw I needed help, but no one helped me."

Vince Vinelli patted the woman's hand. Then he turned to the camera and pointed his finger directly at Charlie.

"Viewers! When crime is a fact, good people act! Why didn't anyone act? Where were the good people? Remember . . ." Vince Vinelli took a deep breath and boomed out his signature line, the one he encouraged his audience to say with him.

"Good people do good things!"

The phone number flashed on the television screen along with pictures of wanted criminals.

"Irving!" Grandma Tickler leaned over and poked Grandpa Tickler. "Do any of those criminals look familiar?"

"Ayuh," Grandpa Ticker said.

"I didn't think so," Grandma Tickler agreed.

Grandma Tickler turned off the TV and shuffled upstairs with Grandpa Tickler. Where were those crime-fighting grandparents from this morning?

Charlie followed them slowly up the stairs. He doubted Grandma and Grandpa Tickler's self-defense moves would be effective against a criminal who was not moving at the speed of mud.

Charlie brushed his teeth and in the mirror repeated the sign Aggie had used. He rinsed his mouth and wiped up the toothpaste in the sink.

No one came to tuck him in.

Charlie checked the closet for wanted criminals. Then he turned off the ceiling light and made a running leap for his bed. He made sure to begin his jump far enough away to clear any arms that might stretch out from under his bed and grab him.

With his bedside lamp on, Charlie pulled the covers up to his chin. He reached for his library book. Then he glanced at his dresser, where Aggie's bag rested.

*When crime is a fact, good people act.*

Had a crime been committed? Charlie didn't know. He only knew that Aggie had been afraid.

*Good people do good things.*

Charlie sighed.

He would ride the gondola across the Hudson River.

He would find Frog Castle.

He would find out what that sign meant.

# 7. Genius

"Is this safe? No way this is safe."

"I'm sure it's perfectly safe."

It was the same young couple Charlie had passed by yesterday. They stood next to Charlie, waiting to board the gondola along with other tourists huddled together clutching cell phones and laptops.

Charlie watched the gondola glide across a narrow span of the Hudson River on a steel cable. Mr. Simple controlled the gondola from inside the station on the riverfront. He cranked gears, pulled levers, and pushed buttons.

"This is a one-man operation?" the guy asked.

"That doesn't seem right. I want to see an inspection certificate—you know, like they have with elevators."

"Would you stop? It's the fastest way to get there. Besides, they have cell phone service and Wi-Fi up at the castle—a castle!" The woman sighed. "Just like in England!"

The gondola pulled into the station, and a group of queasy-looking passengers disembarked. Mr. Simple collected dollar bills from the passengers waiting to board.

Charlie stepped out of line and took a few deep breaths.

"You riding?" Mr. Simple asked Charlie. Mr. Simple's forearms were huge. Popeye huge.

Charlie nodded hesitantly.

"Don't worry. I've been operating this gondola over forty years. Never lost anyone yet." He winked at Charlie.

Charlie took a deep breath and handed Mr. Simple four quarters. Mr. Simple handed Charlie a US Mail bag in exchange.

"Give this to Oliver, would you? He'll be the lad meeting you on the other side."

Mr. Simple locked the door and returned to the controls. The gondola began to inch forward and upward, higher and higher, until it was swinging over the Hudson River. The castle sat on a bluff, its turrets and towers dark against the bright blue sky. Sailboats dotted the Hudson, glittering in the sunshine below.

Charlie had just begun to relax when the gondola came to a sudden stop.

The cabin swayed left and right and then slid quickly backward.

"Help," someone whispered.

Charlie clutched the mailbag to his chest. The gondola jerked. Charlie's stomach flipped. Several people squealed. Charlie pictured Mr. Simple inside the station, gleefully playing with gears and levers and buttons. Then, as if Mr. Simple felt he had tortured them enough, the gondola moved smoothly forward again. A sigh of relief echoed around the cabin as the journey resumed.

A small crowd was waiting to take the return trip. A man unlocked the gondola door. A thin kid wearing a green-and-gold Castle Bullfrogs T-shirt placed a step stool in the doorway.

The kid held out a hand for passengers who needed assistance. "Welcome to Castle School for the Deaf!" he yelled. "Head right up to the Flying Hands Café with free—yes, free!—high-speed Internet. The food is delicious, thanks to our world-renowned chef! The café is a sign-language-only environment. Good luck, hearing people!"

Charlie stepped off the stool. He was never so glad to be on solid ground again.

"Are you Oliver?" Charlie asked.

"That would be me."

"This is for you. It's from Mr. Simple."

Oliver reached into the mailbag and pulled out one letter. "Give this to my mother, would you? She's the woman running the café. Thanks." Oliver handed the letter to Charlie and turned to the waiting crowd to help them board. Charlie looked at the letter.

*Nathan Marsh*
*Nathan's Ice Cream Emporium*
*Castle-on-the-Hudson, NY*

*Eleanor Castle*
*Castle School for the Deaf*

"Sure," Charlie said. Why not? Since he had arrived in Castle-on-the-Hudson, people had been handing him things: a key, a library book, a knitting bag, a mailbag—and Charlie had taken them all.

He followed the crowd up to the castle. Next to the massive front doors was an engraved plaque that read:

CASTLE SCHOOL FOR THE DEAF
FOUNDED 1818

Charlie stepped into a domed foyer. The Flying Hands Café was on the right. Some of the gondola passengers had obviously been here before. They went right inside and sat down. But several others, like Charlie, stood in the front, unsure of what to do next.

No one was talking in the café. Everyone was signing, texting, or tapping on a keyboard.

A tall woman in a billowy skirt handed Charlie a menu. She gestured for him to read it.

WELCOME TO THE FLYING
HANDS CAFÉ!
We communicate in American Sign Language (ASL) but feel free to use any other sign language you know: French Sign Language, Japanese Sign Language, Kenyan Sign Language, etc.
If you use your voice to communicate while in our café, you will pay the price on the left side of the menu. If you use your hands to communicate, you will pay the price on the right side of the menu.

Charlie looked at the prices.

If you used your hands to communicate, a glass of lemonade was $1.99.

If you used your voice, a glass of lemonade was $4.99.

All your servers are Deaf.
Please use the back of the menu to learn the manual alphabet and basic signs in ASL.
Pointing also works. And smiling. ☺
Enjoy!

The woman raised her eyebrows as if to say, "You got it?"

It wasn't really a question. It was more of a warning. Charlie bet this was Oliver's mother. He showed her the letter. She took it and gave Charlie a thumbs-up.

Charlie sat in a booth by a window and took in the smells of roast chicken, macaroni and cheese, and fudge brownies. Or at least that's what he thought he smelled. But first Charlie needed something to drink. He turned to the back of the menu and practiced the signs *"I,"* *"want,"* and *"drink."*

A girl came over and stood by Charlie's booth. She wore the same Flying Hands Café black T-shirt and apron as the other servers. But she also wore a diamond brooch the size and shape of a daisy. She couldn't be a server, though. She looked the same age as Charlie. She tapped her pen impatiently on her notepad and gave Charlie a let's-hurry-this-up look.

Charlie pointed at her and fingerspelled WAITER?

The girl pointed at Charlie and spelled back GENIUS! She touched the middle finger of her open hand to her forehead and flicked her palm out as her hand moved away. *"Genius."*

That was rude. And was it even legal to wait tables at her age? Charlie repeated the sign with his left hand. *"Genius."*

The girl scribbled on her pad of paper.

*Sorry. In a bad mood. My mother is making me crazy!*

She looked pointedly at Oliver's mother. Charlie nodded. He understood about mothers making you crazy. He signed, *"I want a drink,"* and pointed to the word "lemonade." The girl nodded. She was about to turn away when Charlie gestured to her paper and pen.

Charlie wrote: *I'm looking for someone named Frog.*

The girl pointed to herself.

Charlie pointed back at her with a look that said "That's you?"

Frog signed, *"Genius!"* and pointed at Charlie. But this time she grinned.

Frog wrote: *I'm Francine Castle, aka Frog. Why are you looking for me?*

*Can you please tell me what this sign means?* Charlie asked.

Charlie put down the paper and pen. He showed Frog the sign Aggie had used in the library. He held his hands out in front of him with one palm up and the other palm down. Then he flipped his hands over. One palm down and the other palm up.

Frog gave him an odd look, then translated: DEAD.

# 8. Dead

Dead.

"*Dead*" was what Aggie had signed.

*Why do you want to know the sign for "dead"?*
Frog asked.

Charlie explained what had happened at the library
with Aggie and Miss Tweedy, and Dex and Ray. Frog
immediately assessed the situation.

*Obviously Dex and Ray were looking for the same
thing Aggie was looking for,* Frog concluded. *But what did
Aggie mean when she said she told a secret? And what did
she mean when she said theft, destruction, or worse would
happen unless she fixed it?*

*I don't know,* Charlie wrote.

*Why don't you know? You should have asked her when you had the chance!*

*Aggie was upset! It didn't seem appropriate to ask questions.*

*Appropriate?*

*Appropriate means—*

Frog grabbed the pen. *I know what it means! That wasn't the time for APPROPRIATE! It was the time for action! To ask hard questions! To discover the truth!*

Charlie didn't know what to say. Instead he wrote: *Miss Tweedy said she's fluent in American Sign Language. But she had never seen the sign "dead" before.*

Frog snorted.

*Miss Tweedy hates anything to do with death! She refused to learn that sign when I was teaching her. Besides, she's only fluent in Tweedy Sign Language—TSL.*

*Then is this the sign for "wrong"?* Charlie asked. *Miss Tweedy said it was.*

Charlie showed Frog the sign.

Frog nodded. *Yes, it is. Sometimes Miss Tweedy does get ASL right! She forgets easily, though, so you have to be patient with her. Okay, writing is way too slow! Be right back!*

Frog signed something to her mother and left the café. Charlie still had no lemonade.

The people next to Charlie had stopped

texting each other with their phones. They were now whisper-arguing. Frog's mother went over to their table. She jabbed her finger at the higher prices on the left side of the menu. They closed their mouths and resumed text-arguing.

Frog returned with Oliver and gestured for Charlie to follow them. Charlie tried to sign, *"I want a drink,"* but they were already walking out of the café.

The domed foyer opened onto a great hall with a vaulted ceiling and enormous windows. Paintings, portraits, and glass exhibit cases lined the walls. In the middle of the great hall stood a statue of two girls. At the far end of the hall a woman was hanging a large banner that read:

WELCOME TO

CASTLE SCHOOL FOR THE DEAF

FOUNDERS' DAY DINNER

Frog and Oliver headed toward the wide stone staircase leading to the upper floors of the castle. Charlie trailed them up the stairs to a landing overlooking the great hall. Two passageways ran on either side of the landing. They turned down the left passage and walked to a door leading into an apartment.

They passed by a living room, a dining room, and

a kitchen, where the refrigerator was surely filled with cold drinks.

Frog marched them into a bedroom. Clothes lay scattered on the floor, along with books and pens and papers. The dresser top glittered with piles of jewelry. And there were frogs. Frogs everywhere. Frog posters, frog figurines, frog pillows, frog lamps, frog stuffed animals, and a frog picture frame with a photograph of Frog as a toddler. She was squatting like a frog, looking at the camera with big eyes and a wide smile.

Frog gestured for Charlie to sit on the book-covered bed. Charlie pushed aside *The Adventures of Sherlock Holmes*, *The Secret Garden*, and *The Complete Book of Poisons* and sat down.

Oliver plopped down next to Charlie. Frog dragged a chair from the desk in the corner and sat facing them both. Watching Oliver closely, Frog began signing.

*"This is my brother Oliver,"* Frog signed as Oliver spoke. *"He's going to interpret for us. He'd better say exactly what I sign and not add any of his own opinions or I will become infuriated and hit him."*

"Okay, she didn't really say that last part," Oliver added while also signing, "but that's what she meant. And for the record I'm her older brother."

Frog leaned forward and gave Oliver a punch on the arm.

"Ow!" Oliver said.

Frog continued signing and Oliver continued interpreting.

*"The answer is yes,"* Frog said.

Frog looked expectantly at Charlie, waiting for his response.

"Um," Charlie said. "What's the question?"

*"Will I help you solve this mystery?"*

"What mystery?" Charlie asked.

*"The murder mystery!"*

"There is no murder mystery!"

*"You just said that woman Aggie signed 'dead' to you!"*

"Yes!" Charlie said. "But that doesn't mean someone was murdered!"

*"She told a secret that she obviously wasn't supposed to tell,"* Frog said. *"Then she told you something about death. Something is clearly wrong. Murder wrong!"*

"Look," Charlie said. "Maybe Aggie meant, 'I'm dead tired.' Or she meant, 'There's a deadly animal outside!'"

*"The meaning of 'dead' is different in those examples, so the sign used would be different. I think something is really wrong, and if something is really wrong, do you want to do nothing? Good people do good things."*

"Vince Vinelli?" Charlie said. "You watch Vince Vinelli, too?"

Frog pointed to a picture on her wall. Like a prince

among frogs, there hung Vince Vinelli and his gleaming white teeth. Pointing a finger right at Charlie.

*"V-V!"* Frog signed and kissed the back of her fist.

*"Vince Vinelli says good people act,"* Frog told Charlie. *"He means us! We have to act!"*

"We could tell the police," Charlie said.

*"Tell them what? That a woman signed 'dead' to you and then disappeared? We need to find Dex and Ray. We need to find out what crime they committed."*

"I don't know that they committed any crime," Charlie said. "I only know Aggie was scared."

*"We need to find Aggie, then,"* Frog said. *"We need to find out what she was trying to tell you."*

"True," Oliver signed and said. Frog did not punch him this time.

Charlie considered.

Aggie had needed help from Charlie. She had signed to *him.* But he couldn't help her because he didn't understand sign language. Charlie looked at Vince Vinelli.

*Good people do good things.*

"Let's do it," Charlie said.

# 9. I Will

*"If we're going to solve a murder mystery together, you need to learn ASL,"* Frog told Charlie as Oliver interpreted.

"Can we just call it a 'mystery'?" Charlie asked. "Or call it 'helping Aggie'?"

*"I plan to be a detective,"* Frog said, *"so I prefer to call it a murder mystery. It'll look better on my résumé."*

"Arguing with Frog is pointless," Oliver told Charlie. "Besides, James or Millie should be the ones teaching you ASL. James isn't here. Millie is only six, but she's got way more patience than Frog has." Oliver then signed what he had just said to Frog. Frog fingerspelled two words to him slowly and deliberately.

GO AWAY.

Oliver stood up. "Good luck, Charlie." Oliver gave him a pat on the shoulder. "You're going to need it."

Frog pulled out her notepad and pen as Charlie heard the front door slam shut.

*Oliver is such a pain!* Frog wrote.

*At least he interpreted for us*, Charlie responded.

*He has to interpret. I know his secret. This is the price for my silence.*

Charlie heard the front door open again, which he signaled to Frog. Nails click-clacked along the hallway floor. In the doorway stood a small girl and a large black bear. Actually, it was a dog that looked like a black bear. The dog held a rolled-up piece of paper in its mouth. Frog reached for the drool-covered paper with her thumb and forefinger.

*Frog! Get back here now! Mom.*

Frog scribbled a response as the bear-dog panted with a bright pink tongue.

Frog handed the note to the dog and then wiped her hands on her shorts. The dog trotted out of the room. The little girl followed. Charlie heard the front door open and close once more.

Frog was now searching for a book on her shelves.

The girl returned and tapped Frog on the shoulder. Frog signed something.

"Oh, you're hearing," the girl said to Charlie. "I'm Millie. What's your name?"

"Charlie," Charlie said. Millie was also "hearing," and she had two missing front teeth.

"Hi, Charlie. Frog's been gone too long. Mom didn't trust she would read Bear's note, so she sent me to make sure Frog came back. The café is really busy today."

Café. Lemonade.

"Millie," Charlie said, "may I *please* have a glass of water?"

"Sure!"

Millie came back with water. Charlie drank the entire glass as Frog shoved a book into Charlie's free hand.

*Dorrie McCann and the Mystery of the Secret Treasure* by D. J. McKinnon. A girl stared at Charlie from the front cover: arms crossed, eyes in a steely-eyed squint, ready to solve a mystery.

"Frog loves those books," Millie told Charlie as Frog focused on her notepad. "Dorrie is Deaf and she solves mysteries. Frog wants to be a detective. I do, too! Did you know my dog Bear is a Newfoundland? Newfs are one of the biggest dogs in the world."

Frog showed Charlie what she had written.

*Read this book!!! Learn some sign with Millie before you*

*leave!!! Meet me at the library tomorrow at 11:00 a.m.!!!*

Geez, Frog sure means business, Charlie thought. And she sure loved exclamation points.

*I will!!!* Charlie wrote.

Frog showed Charlie how to sign *"I will."* She moved a flat hand from the side of her chin straight outward. *"I will."*

Charlie started to copy what she signed, then stopped. He realized he was using his left hand when Frog was using her right. Did it matter?

Frog shook her head. *It doesn't matter. You're left-handed, so just do the opposite of me. Whatever my right hand does, you sign with your left. Whatever my left hand does, you sign with your right. Now show me!*

Charlie signed, *"I will."*

Frog shook her head and scowled. Clearly Charlie was doing it wrong—*"wrong"* Charlie signed in his head. Finally Charlie must have done it right because Frog nodded and motioned for them to go downstairs.

Oliver was right. Frog was not a patient teacher. Though Frog had said she was patient with Miss Tweedy. As he walked behind Frog and Millie, Charlie practiced the sign *"I will."* He hoped he wouldn't forget it. He had a feeling Frog would be quizzing him later on.

• • •

*Vince Vinelli's Worst Criminals Ever!* was not on TV that night. Grandma and Grandpa Tickler watched a baking competition show instead. Charlie sat on the sofa with the book Frog had ordered him to read: *Dorrie McCann and the Mystery of the Secret Treasure* by D. J. McKinnon.

Charlie leafed through the book. Then he tossed it aside to practice the signs Millie had taught him.

*"Ice cream."* That was easy to remember. It looked like someone licking an ice cream cone. Tomorrow he would show Frog the new signs he had learned. Frog would be impressed—Charlie was certain.

"Irving! That angel food cake looks too flat, don't you agree?" Grandma Tickler shouted during a commercial.

"Ayuh," Grandpa Tickler agreed.

Yvette, who was cleaning up the kitchen, strolled into the living room.

"He didn't beat his egg whites enough," Yvette said. She went back into the kitchen. The contestant who baked the angel food cake was voted out.

"It should have been fluffier," Grandma Tickler said. "It didn't look good."

"Ayuh," Grandpa Tickler said.

As usual, Grandma Tickler understood immediately Grandpa Tickler's "ayuh." And in this case, she disagreed.

"How can a cake be good if it doesn't look good, Irving?" Grandma Tickler demanded.

A commercial came on. Grandma Tickler stretched her arms and did a little twist in her E-Z chair recliner. She noticed Charlie sitting on the sofa.

"We haven't done much for Charlie since Alistair and Myra left," Grandma Tickler said to Grandpa Tickler. "Didn't we do things for Alistair when he was Charlie's age?"

"Ayuh," Grandpa Tickler said.

"I thought so," Grandma Tickler said. "Yvette! Does Charlie need us to do anything?"

Yvette came out of the kitchen.

"He's right here, Irma. Charlie, do you need anything?" Yvette asked, wiping her hands on a dishcloth.

Yes.

Yes, he needed things.

He needed lots of things.

He needed a new toothbrush.

He needed new socks.

He needed parents who wanted him along as they helped.

He needed grandparents who wanted him to stay.

"No," Charlie said.

"There you go," Yvette said. The baking competition show came back on. Yvette turned to go into the kitchen.

"Yvette?" Charlie said.

"Yes?"

Charlie looked over at his grandparents. "Do you think people can be like that angel food cake? They may not look good, but they could still be good?"

Yvette eyed Grandma and Grandpa Tickler.

"In my experience, Charlie," Yvette said, "what you see is what you get."

# 10. Blood

The cat was sitting by the front door of the library. Mr. Dickens eyed Charlie with disdain.

"Say good morning to Mr. Dickens," Miss Tweedy called, "otherwise he gets in a mood."

Mr. Dickens looked like he was already in a mood, but Charlie reached down to pet him nonetheless. "Good morning, Mr. Dickens."

"No petting!" Miss Tweedy screeched as Mr. Dickens swiped his claws at Charlie. "Mr. Dickens only likes to be petted in the afternoon," Miss Tweedy explained. "Feel free to pet him after one o'clock."

"Okay," Charlie said. He would not be petting Mr. Dickens any time of day. Charlie approached the circulation desk.

"Miss Tweedy, do you have grandchildren?"

"I have not been so blessed," Miss Tweedy said. "I have, however, been a grandchild."

"Did your grandparents do things with you?" Charlie asked.

"Oh, yes!" Miss Tweedy said. "I have the most marvelous memories of my grandfather reading to me. I remember one book quite vividly."

"Which book?" Charlie asked.

Miss Tweedy walked over to a pile of books and plucked one out. *Great Expectations* by Charles Dickens.

The book was yellowed and musty. But Miss Tweedy smiled so fondly at it (and the author's name *was* Charles) that Charlie decided to try it.

"Library card, please," Miss Tweedy said. Despite typing the library card for Charlie only yesterday, Miss Tweedy inspected it thoroughly. Only then did she check the book out to Charlie. He had just settled into a worn overstuffed armchair in the front of the library when Frog strode through the door. Mr. Dickens peered around the corner and eyed her with vigilance.

The daisy diamond brooch from yesterday was gone. Today, cherry-size rubies hung from Frog's ears. She pulled out a pen and notepad from the leather bag slung across her body, and flopped into the armchair next to Charlie's. The rubies shimmied. Frog breathed in deeply and smiled.

*I like the smell of the library,* Frog wrote. *Did you read Dorrie McCann yet?*

*You just gave it to me yesterday!* Charlie wrote back.

*Well, make sure you read it ASAP!* Frog settled into her chair. *Now show me the signs Millie taught you.*

Charlie had been waiting for this. He carefully signed: "*dog*," "*cat*," "*yes*," "*no*," "*good*," "*bad*," "*can*," "*can't*," "*tree*," "*flower*," "*grass*," "*water*," "*ice cream*," "*cookie*," "*mom*," "*dad*," "*hearing*," "*Deaf*," and the numbers one through ten. Charlie even made sure he signed the numbers one through five with his palm facing toward him, and then turned his palm outward for the rest of the numbers.

Frog stared at him with an incredulous look.

Wait. He had forgotten one sign—"*happy.*"

There. Why wasn't Frog saying anything? Charlie wondered.

*What's wrong?* he wrote.

*How are those signs good for solving a murder mystery?!*

*Millie's six!* Charlie wrote. *She didn't know how to teach me! So finally I asked her how to sign some words I thought a six-year-old would know! And can't we just call it a mystery?*

Frog glanced up toward the ceiling with a look that said "Why is my life so hard?"

She grabbed the pen and wrote: *Now learn these signs: "blood," "kill," "poison," "stab," "shoot," "hide," "body," "library," "investigate," "who," "what," "when," "where," "why." You already know "dead" and "wrong," so I suppose you should learn the signs "alive" and "right."*

Frog started with the sign for "*blood.*" Palm facing in, she brushed her right index finger down her lips. Then she opened her right hand, and wiggled her fingers downward over her left open hand.

When Frog was satisfied with how Charlie had signed everything, she wrote: *Ready to start our investigation?*

"*Yes,*" Charlie signed. See? Millie *had* taught him some useful signs.

*Good! Let's see if there is a dead body in the library.*

# 11. That

Charlie and Frog climbed the oak staircase to the children's section, a large sunny room overlooking Main Street. They checked under fat pillows and behind a stuffed lion. They explored four other high-ceilinged rooms crammed with books, peering into chimneys, searching under tables and armchairs. They continued their investigation downstairs. When they reached the section Aggie had gone to when she first entered the library, Charlie stopped Frog.

Frog's eyes scanned the shelves:

*Nonfiction 929–956 Genealogy, Ancient History, World History…Reference 000–999…Nonfiction 327–339*

*Political Science, Economics, Financial Planning . . .*
*Nonfiction 340–364 Law, Military, Criminology . . .*

Frog pointed to "Criminology" with a knowing look. She wrote: *Aggie signed "dead." Crime books usually involve death. It makes sense she was looking here.*

But if Aggie had been looking for a book in the criminology section, how would they know which book? They examined some of the titles: *Enemies Within, Inside the Criminal Mind, Why Good People Go Bad.* Nothing seemed obvious.

*Maybe,* Charlie wrote, *Aggie signed "dead" because she was upset someone she loved just died. Maybe someone rich. She was looking for a book to help her.*

*In criminology?!*

Charlie pointed to a book in the financial planning section: *Suddenly Rich! What to Do When Someone Leaves You a Pile of Money.*

Frog took a minute to answer. *How does that connect with the secret she told? And fixing what she did before theft or destruction or worse happens? And that Dex and Ray are looking for her because she knows where "it" is?*

*It doesn't,* Charlie admitted.

Frog signed the letter *Y,* and then moved her arm downward from her elbow.

*This sign means "that." In English you could say, "That's what I mean!"*

Charlie copied the sign. *"That."*

Charlie then showed Frog the window where Aggie had climbed out. Like Charlie, Frog was impressed Aggie had made the jump.

Miss Tweedy was the next stop in their investigation. She had pink lipstick on her front teeth again. Unlike Charlie, Frog immediately pointed this out. Miss Tweedy rubbed her teeth with her finger.

Charlie watched their exchange carefully. Miss Tweedy *did* use her hands and body to tell her version of what happened, but even Charlie could tell she was not using American Sign Language.

Miss Tweedy's hands swooped and swelled. They fluttered and flurried. She danced on her tiptoes over to the front windows and gestured fiercely. She tapped her collarbone, pointed at Mr. Dickens, and jabbed a finger at Charlie. She ended her story with a leap and a pirouette. The out-of-breath Miss Tweedy bowed. She tapped her collarbone once more, and went through the door behind the circulation desk.

*Same thing you told me*, Frog wrote.

*You understood that? How?*

*I've known Miss Tweedy my whole life—I'm fluent in TSL. She went to visit Mrs. Murphy and left you to run the library.*

Frog's eyes searched the library and landed on the portrait of the pink-shirted man hanging above the fireplace.

*Mr. Woo was the librarian*, Frog wrote.

Frog paused meaningfully.

*Until he died last month. Suddenly.*

*That's awful!*

Frog agreed. *That could be the reason Aggie came to the library! Maybe Aggie knows a secret about Mr. Woo—a secret he shared with her! Now Mr. Woo is DEAD. How did Mr. Woo REALLY die? We need to check the morgue!*

*Or,* Charlie wrote, *Aggie came here for a book. She did come to a library, after all.* Charlie was not going to the morgue. He just wanted to find Aggie and make sure she was okay.

Frog sighed and thought for a moment. She made a decision.

*Blythe and Bone Bookshop. That's where we go next to investigate books AND the possible murder of Harold Woo.*

*"Okay,"* Charlie signed. He did not ask why. At least it was a bookshop and not a morgue.

*And we look for Aggie,* Charlie added.

*"That,"* Frog signed. That's what I mean.

Charlie hoped so.

# 12. Impossible

The villagers of Castle-on-the-Hudson sure loved coffee. Charlie noticed café after café as they walked: Coffee Cup, Coffee Pot, Coffee Cake, Coffee & Cream.

Frog wrote: *We're famous for the most coffee shops per square block!*

Frog inhaled the coffee-scented air and kissed the back of her fist. Charlie peered into each café window searching for Aggie. He made sure his key was still in his pocket.

*"What?"* Frog signed.

*It's my key,* Charlie wrote. *Just in case.*

Frog understood. *Vince Vinelli*. She nodded. *Good idea.*

Frog pointed to a store called Junk and Stuff. A silver-haired woman wearing huge diamond earrings was writing a note to the clerk inside. The clerk read her note and shook his head. The silver-haired woman frowned and snatched the note back. Charlie looked past the woman and the clerk. Yep—lots of stuff, most of it junk.

Frog peered in as well.

*Love her earrings! This store is where I buy all of my statement pieces.*

*Statement pieces?*

*My fantastic jewelry!* Frog pointed to her ruby earrings. *They make a statement about me!*

*They do?*

*Of course they do! They say I'm unique!*

Charlie did not need jewelry to tell him that Frog was unique.

*You should consider a statement piece*, Frog told Charlie. *Wear special sneakers or some kind of T-shirt.*

*Right*, Charlie wrote.

*How do you decide what to wear every day?*

*I reach in my drawer and pull something out. I put it on.*

*That's no good. We need to find your style.*

*We need to find Aggie*, Charlie wrote.

•  •  •

As they walked, Charlie practiced signing. Frog corrected Charlie's mistakes while steering him around dog bowls and benches. In between correcting and steering, Frog managed to say hello to most of the village. She knew everyone—the three kids riding bikes, the shopkeeper sweeping the sidewalk, the boy on the skateboard, the woman watering the flower baskets hanging on lampposts, the girl jumping rope. If they were Deaf, Frog signed. If they could hear, Frog either signed or gestured or wrote notes. Frog told Charlie that besides saying hello, which was only polite, she was also asking if they had seen Aggie.

No one had.

Frog stopped in front of an ivy-covered cottage with a purple front door.

### DESDEMONA FINKELSTEIN, F.T.E.
#### CASH ONLY
#### OPEN 10–4
#### (UNLESS THE UNIVERSE TELLS ME DIFFERENTLY)

*Desdemona may have information for us*, Frog wrote. Frog tried the brass doorknob. Closed.
*What kind of information?* Charlie asked.
*Vital information*, Frog answered.

*What does that mean?*

*Vital means important*, Frog wrote with a smug look.

*I know what "vital" means! What kind of vital information? Who is she?*

Frog ignored Charlie's question.

Instead she wrote: *We'll come back when she's here.*

*When's that?*

*How should I know? Desdemona only works when the universe tells her to work.*

Charlie stopped asking questions.

• • •

Blythe and Bone Bookshop was a stately brick building. A young woman with a cloud of curly hair was arranging books in the large front window. She spotted Frog and grinned. They signed to each other as Frog stood on the sidewalk and the woman knelt in the window display. Charlie liked that it didn't matter if one person was outside and the other person was inside. As long as you could see each other, you could carry on your conversation.

When Charlie and Frog opened the shop door, a lamp flashed on and off at the desk where an old man was writing. The man looked up when the lamp flickered on. Then he scowled and returned to his papers.

Blythe and Bone Bookshop, unlike the Castle-on-the-Hudson Library, was orderly and elegant, with neatly shelved books and polished wood tables and chairs. Coffee and tea brewed behind the counter. Customers sipped from porcelain cups as they browsed and read. Charlie recognized the young couple from the gondola yesterday. The woman was flipping through a book on country castles. The man was engrossed in a book called *Gondolas: Transportation or Terror?*

Frog hugged the woman from the window display, pointed to Charlie, then fingerspelled his name. The young woman turned to Charlie and stuck out her hand. On her brown skin was a tattoo of a little girl reading a book. Underneath were the words "You are not alone."

"Nice to meet you, Charlie. I'm Matilda Blythe. And that grumpy gentleman over there is my grandfather, Thelonious Bone." Matilda jerked a thumb toward the man sitting at the desk, whom Frog was now approaching. "Frog wants to talk to Bone about Harold Woo. This should be interesting. Don't worry, I'll interpret."

Frog pulled up a chair and sat across from Bone. Bone would not look up. Finally he glared at Frog out of the corner of his eye.

Frog immediately signed, *"Do you mind if I ask some questions about Mr. Woo?"*

Matilda interpreted Frog's question in a sweet voice

because right now Frog did look very sweet. And very un-Frog-like.

Bone snapped his hands at her. *"Yes, I mind, you impertinent child!"* Matilda made her grandfather's voice sound raspy and gruff.

*"But it's important,"* Frog insisted. *"You're the one who found Mr. Woo. I need to know exactly how Mr. Woo died."*

Bone waved Frog away with a flick of his hand.

Frog gazed at Bone with an angelic look and folded her hands in her lap.

Matilda nodded approvingly. "Brilliant. Now Frog waits. If she waits long enough, Bone will talk." Matilda moved around the counter. "Coffee?" she asked, pouring herself a cup. "No? All right, then. Why all the questions about Harold Woo and how he died?"

"Well," Charlie began. What could Charlie say to Matilda that Frog wouldn't mind him sharing? "Harold Woo died so suddenly—"

"Suddenly? He was ninety-nine years old!"

"He was?"

"Granted he was the most active ninety-nine-year-old I'd ever met. But he was ninety-nine! Somehow the village was gobsmacked he didn't make it to one hundred. Especially Miss Tweedy. She had all these 'Congratulations! You're One Hundred Years Old!' party decorations she had purchased. I suggested cutting off the extra zeros and finding a nine-year-old who was about to have a birthday. She was not amused."

Did Frog *really* think Harold Woo had been poisoned? Charlie wondered. Or was she just trying to find any reason for Aggie to have signed "*dead*"?

Charlie changed the subject.

"How did you learn sign language?" he asked. "From your grandfather?"

"My parents are also Deaf," Matilda said. "So I'm bilingual—I learned to sign before I could speak— Oh, look! Bone's ready to talk."

Bone capped his pen. He itched his ear. He played with a paper clip.

"*You're still here,*" Bone signed to Frog as Matilda interpreted for Charlie.

"*Yes I am,*" Frog said.

"*Why,*" Bone asked, "*do you want to know about Harold Woo?*"

"*I just want to make sure he died of natural causes.*"

"*Harold Woo died,*" Bone said, "*the best way possible— reading a book.* Something Wicked This Way Comes. *It was lying on his chest when I found him.*"

Frog perked up at the book title.

"*Isn't that suspicious?*" Frog said. "*That he was reading* that *book when he died? Maybe Mr. Woo was sending you a message.*"

*"Message? What message?"* Bone's bow tie quivered.

*"A message,"* Frog said, *"that his death was not what it appeared to be."* Frog sat calmly in her chair and let that sink in. Bone's face turned red.

*"What are you saying?"*

Frog narrowed her eyes as she leaned closer to Bone. *"I'm saying . . . maybe Mr. Woo was poisoned."*

Mr. Bone pushed off the desk and stood.

*"Impossible!"* Bone signed the letter *Y* and smacked it twice on the palm of his opposite hand. He jerked his suit jacket off the back of his chair while Charlie practiced the sign. *"Impossible."*

*"Why?"* Frog asked. *"Many poisons are undetectable."*

*"Rude, rude girl!"* Bone stomped out of the bookshop.

Matilda turned to Charlie. "Frog thinks Harold was *murdered*?"

"I'm sure it's a misunderstanding," Charlie said vaguely. He tried changing the subject again. "Matilda, do you have a criminology section? And a financial planning section? Frog and I are looking for a book."

# 13. Boring

Charlie and Frog stared at the bowl of ice cream with bright green flecks in it.

"See, it's butterscotch ice cream," Nate of Nathan's Ice Cream Emporium explained, "but with *broccoli* in it." Nate haltingly signed and at the same time spoke in a hoarse-sandpapery voice. "No more telling kids they have to eat their vegetables before they get dessert. The vegetables *are* the dessert. Butterscotch. Broccoli. Ice cream."

Frog leaned back on her stool as if butterscotch broccoli ice cream were contagious.

"Why can't vegetables and ice cream go together?" Nate continued. "Why does it have to be one or the other? I'm a hard-of-hearing man in the hearing world *and* I'm a Deaf man with a little hearing in the Deaf world. I'm not one or the other—I'm both! Because Deaf people come all different ways—just like ice cream."

Frog didn't understand what Nate was saying. So he stopped speaking English while using signs, and instead tried communicating in ASL to explain his vegetable ice cream theory.

This time Frog nodded. Then she arched an eyebrow at Nate.

"Come on, Frog," Nate said and signed. "You're only going to eat coffee ice cream the rest of your life? That's boring!"

Charlie liked the sign for "boring": Nate placed the side of his index finger next to his nose, and then twisted it so his palm faced inward. "*Boring.*" Maybe butterscotch broccoli ice cream would taste good. Charlie remembered Yvette's meat loaf. He remembered what Grandpa Tickler had said about the angel food cake. It may not look good but it could still be good.

"I'll try it," Charlie said.

"*What?*" Nate signed.

Charlie pointed to the vegetable ice cream and then to himself.

"You'll try it?" Nate said. "Beautiful!"

While Nate went to scoop ice cream, Frog wrote: *Butterscotch broccoli ice cream? You live on the edge, Charlie Tickler.*

*The US Department of Agriculture says vegetables should be eaten daily.*

Frog snorted. *Right.*

Charlie paused. *You don't really think Mr. Woo was poisoned, do you?*

*Detectives keep all possibilities open until they're closed for certain,* Frog wrote. *And until we know for certain, Mr. Woo COULD have been poisoned. Which would explain why Aggie signed "dead" to you in the library. Just saying.*

Nate handed Frog coffee ice cream in a cone and Charlie butterscotch broccoli ice cream in a bowl. Charlie licked a crunchy spoonful. Nate leaned his elbows on the counter and watched. Charlie swirled the ice cream in his mouth. It tasted like chopped-up broccoli mixed with butterscotch ice cream. Except it was hard to appreciate how fantastic the butterscotch tasted with the crunchy broccoli getting in the way. On the other hand, Charlie hadn't eaten a vegetable in a few days.

"Well?" Nate said and signed.

Charlie fingerspelled HEALTHY!

Nate waited for Charlie to continue, so Charlie felt he had to add DELICIOUS!

Nate grinned broadly. "Healthy and delicious—I think I'm onto something."

Frog asked Nate if he had seen a tiny old woman with a black mole on her cheek.

"Nope," Nate said and signed. He wiped the counter with a towel. "But this is the second time I've been asked about her."

Frog and Charlie stopped eating.

"*Who?*" they both signed.

"Two guys," Nate said. "They wanted to know if I'd seen a little old woman with a mole on her cheek. She's their great-aunt and wandered away from home. Not quite right in the head. Why are you asking? You know her?" Nate spoke and then signed this in ASL.

Charlie and Frog glanced at each other. Frog was suddenly busy licking her ice cream while Charlie focused on chewing his.

"What gives?" Nate asked.

Frog smacked her forehead with an I-almost-forgot-something-really-important look and reached into her leather bag. She pulled out an ice cream order for the Founders' Day Dinner.

"Beautiful!" Nate said and signed. "I've been waiting for this!" He scanned the order. "What would your mother think about a few healthy-delicious flavors thrown in? A couple of gallons of chocolate asparagus?

Maybe strawberry spinach? I know—caramel cabbage!"

*"No!"* Frog signed. Another customer came in. Nate went to serve him.

Charlie thought about Dex and Ray telling Nate that Aggie was their great-aunt. He remembered something he had heard Dex say in the library.

*Dex told Ray he had only seen Aggie once before*, Charlie wrote. *On someone named Tony's phone.*

*Who's Tony? And why didn't you tell me this before?*

*I don't know who Tony is. And I didn't tell you because I just remembered!*

Frog shook her head at Charlie's disappointing detective work.

*We should go to the police*, Charlie told Frog. *Dex and Ray are lying. Aggie is not their aunt. And if you think Mr. Woo was poisoned, we should tell them that, too.*

Frog licked her ice cream.

*"What's wrong?"* Charlie signed.

Frog took her pen back. *Okay, I don't really think Mr. Woo was poisoned. But I STILL think it could be a murder mystery! If we go to the police and tell them about Aggie signing "dead," it won't be our investigation anymore. This was going to be MY first murder mystery! It's easy for hearing people to become detectives. It's not that easy if you're Deaf.*

Charlie hadn't thought about that before.

*You'll be an awesome detective,* he told Frog. *There's no way you won't become one.*

"*Thanks,*" Frog said. She bit into her sugar cone with a loud crunch.

*What do you want to be?* Frog asked.

Charlie shrugged. He couldn't think about someday. He had to think about now. He had to think about how to make sure Aggie was safe *and* how not to ruin Frog's first case. He had to think about whether he would soon be sent to boarding school or not.

*Maybe we could just tell the police Aggie is missing so they can look for her,* Charlie wrote. *We can tell them Dex and Ray are looking for her, too. They said she was lost, right? If that's true, I am sure they want help finding her. We don't have to say anything about the secret Aggie told or what Aggie signed to me.*

Frog gave Charlie a thumbs-up and popped the rest of the cone into her mouth. Charlie let his ice cream melt into a butterscotch broccoli puddle.

They went to the cash register. Frog and Nate stared as Charlie, who had spent all the quarters he had riding the gondola, pulled out a one-hundred-dollar bill.

"It was my all my father had," Charlie said. "Can you make change?"

• • •

Out on the sidewalk, Frog reached for her pen.

*I have to get back for my shift after we stop at the police station.*

*It's too bad you have to work so much*, Charlie told her.

*Are you kidding?* Frog wrote. *More work = more money = more books + more jewelry!*

As they passed Coffee, Tea & Me, Charlie glanced in the window. He did this with every shop they passed, to see if Aggie was there. She wasn't.

But Dex and Ray were.

Dex was sipping a cup of coffee. He looked over the rim of his cup just as Charlie was peering through the window. Their eyes met. Without taking his gaze off Charlie, Dex said something to Ray and stood up.

# 14. Police

Charlie grabbed Frog's arm. He fingerspelled DEX as they raced down the sidewalk. Frog looked over her shoulder and came to a sudden stop. She flung open a door and pulled Charlie into Junk and Stuff. The chimes above the door jingled. A pimply-faced teenager was playing an electric guitar behind the counter.

Eyes closed, he warbled along to music—

"Girl, why don't you listen?"

—that only he could hear through his headphones.

Frog's eyes flitted to the jewelry display case before she ran down an aisle. She dove under a rickety table, pulling Charlie with her. They sat with knees to their chests, heads bent, breathing hard. Charlie motioned for Frog's pen and paper.

*Police! We should have run to the police! What's the sign?*

Frog made the letter *C* and tapped it twice near her opposite shoulder. "*Police.*"

*No time!* Frog wrote. *Don't think they saw us, though.*

The front door of Junk and Stuff jingled open.

*They saw us*, Charlie wrote.

"Girl, why don't you care?"

"His voice stinks," Charlie heard Ray say. "Someone ought to tell him."

Charlie and Frog scrunched as small and far back as they could under the table.

Dex and Ray began walking down aisles.

"What a bunch of junk," Ray said.

"Girl, I'm standing right here in front of you!"

The dust under the table tickled Charlie's nose. He clasped his hands over his face and willed the sneeze away.

Dex's and Ray's footsteps came closer.

And closer.

Two pairs of black shoes stood right in front of the table.

Frog's eyes were round and unblinking.

Someone bent down. A face appeared in front of them. Ray.

"Hello," Ray said.

Charlie and Frog did not move.

"Out," Dex said. "Now."

Charlie crawled out from under the table. Frog followed.

"Girl, how can you not see me?"

"You're the kid we met in the library," Dex said. Once again his voice was nice. Polite even. His eyes told a different story.

Sweat dripped down from Charlie's forehead. Frog's eyes were locked on Dex's face.

"We're looking for someone," Dex said. "My aunt. She's somewhere in this village. She's about this tall, has white hair and a black mole on her cheek. Always knitting. You seen her?"

"Girl, open your eyes!"

Charlie shook his head no.

"You sure?" Dex said.

Charlie nodded. A bead of sweat plummeted to the floor.

"Girl, open your ears!"

"How about you?" Dex asked Frog.

Frog shook her head.

"*You're Deaf?*" Dex signed.

Frog's eyes widened. She nodded. Dex signed something else. Frog shook her head harder this time.

Ray moved closer. "I don't believe them," Ray said.

Charlie reached for his key. Before he could pull it out, Dex said, "Enough, Ray."

He studied Charlie and Frog for a moment. "Let's go."

"Just like that? I know they're lying." Ray pulled out a stick of sugar-free cinnamon gum, tossed the wrapper on the floor, and followed after Dex. "Tony's not gonna be happy."

"Girl, I'm begging you, please? Open your heart!"

Ray lifted up the clerk's headphones. "Get a new line of work, kid," Ray advised. "Your voice stinks."

# 15. Bathroom

Castle-on-the-Hudson's police station may have been small, but its chief of police was big. The chief sat with her large feet propped up on her metal desk talking on the phone. Mountains of whirling, blinking, buzzing electronic devices surrounded her. The nameplate on her desk read CHIEF AUGUSTA V. PALEY.

Chief Paley motioned for Charlie and Frog to sit in the two chairs facing her desk. Frog signed the letter *T* and shook it back and forth. She fingerspelled BATHROOM.

Charlie practiced this useful sign as Frog went down a hallway. "*Bathroom*."

"No, sir, I don't concur," Chief Paley shouted into the phone. "I think your argument is fallacious and your attitude is"—the chief picked up a list and scanned it, looking for just the right word—"egregious!"

Chief Paley listened and then said, "I *am* speaking in English, sir." She paused. "No, sir, I am not being disrespectful. I am trying to improve my vocabulary so that— Hello? Sir?"

The chief hung up the phone. "Hey, did you understand what I was saying?" she asked Charlie.

"Sort of," Charlie said.

"My writing teacher said writers need an extensive vocabulary. The problem is, once you have an extensive vocabulary, no one understands you." The chief leaned over her desk and stuck out her hand. "Gus Paley."

"Charlie Tickler." Charlie winced as his fingers were momentarily crushed.

"You're a friend of Frog?"

Charlie liked how that sounded. He wanted very much to be Frog's friend. But wanting it didn't make it so.

"Well," Charlie said, avoiding the question, "I just moved here."

"You couldn't have picked a better place to live. I mean, Deaf people? ASL? This village is awesome! The only downside is we're in the epicenter of the Bermuda Triangle for technology. Cell phone signals, high speed Internet—they all disappear when you're in

Castle-on-the-Hudson. No one can figure it out. I've got all this equipment to crush crime, and I can't use most of it!"

Frog came back. Chief Paley put her feet back on the floor and came around the desk to squish Frog with a hug.

Frog and Chief Paley signed to each other. Charlie watched Chief Paley ask Frog to repeat things. He watched Frog correct Chief Paley each time she signed something wrong. Charlie thought how frustrating it must feel to be around hearing people you can't talk to because they don't know how to sign. And how annoying it must be to always have to teach people your language.

"Okay, I think I got it." Chief Paley turned to Charlie as Frog watched her closely. "There's a Deaf woman named Aggie and two men are trying to find her. The men are claiming they're her nephews and that Aggie wandered away from home. Did I discern Frog's meaning?"

"*Yes,*" Charlie signed. Frog gave Chief Paley a thumbs-up.

"Awesome," Chief Paley said with a fist-pump. "But you don't think Aggie is lost. And you don't think the men are really her nephews. *Why?*" Chief Paley signed and then spoke this question. Frog thought for a moment and then gestured to Charlie to tell the chief. So Charlie told Chief Paley about meeting Aggie on the steps and what had happened inside the library. He didn't tell the chief about what had happened in Junk and Stuff. He didn't want the chief to stop their investigation. He just wanted her to help find Aggie.

"So you don't think the men are her nephews, but you have no proof of this, just what you heard the men say," Chief Paley said. Then she signed to Frog who signed something back. The chief nodded. "And detective intuition," Chief Paley added thoughtfully, "just like Dorrie McCann."

"You read Dorrie McCann?" Charlie asked.

"Of course! Those books are stellar! D. J. McKinnon sure knows how to spin a mystery. I'm learning a ton from her. Did you know D. J. McKinnon was also a printer?"

Frog signed something to Chief Paley. "Right." Chief Paley nodded. "Frog wants me to explain to you that D.J. printed the old-fashioned way—with a roller that pressed paper onto inked metal letters, set into place by hand. Here's a cool fact: D.J. printed the first Dorrie McCann books herself! And her protagonist is amazing. Deaf can! That's Dorrie McCann's motto."

Frog signed to Chief Paley, who turned to Charlie. "What? You promised to read a Dorrie McCann mystery and you haven't yet?"

"I will read it!" Charlie said. "It's only been one day!"

Charlie wrote this down for Frog, who rolled her eyes.

Chief Paley signed and then said, "If their aunt Aggie is really lost, they should have filed an MPR—that's Missing Persons Report for you civilians. I'll tell you what—you give me a description and I'll take a look around the village for Aggie, Dex, and Ray. See if we can figure out what's going on. Nice job being proactive citizens." Chief Paley held out a fist for each of them to bump. "Remember—good people do good things!"

"Oh no," Charlie said. "Not you, too."

"Definitely me, too," Chief Paley said. She pointed to a framed photo on the wall—Vince Vinelli and his gleaming teeth.

Chief Paley and Frog both kissed the back of their fists.

# 16. Careful

Charlie waited in line with Frog next to two gondola first-timers.

"This seems really dangerous," one said.

"You're exaggerating."

The gondola wrenched to a stop. It swung and swayed over the Hudson River for several long seconds. Finally it pitched forward again.

"Am I?" the first friend said. "Am I?"

Frog watched their faces and body language as Charlie wondered what the Department of Transportation statistics were for gondola deaths each year. Frog read his mind because she wrote: *The gondola is totally safe! Much safer than driving a car!*

But Charlie felt better now that Chief Paley knew about Aggie. And he knew Frog was happy the Aggie case was still her (and Charlie's) investigation.

*Remember*, Frog wrote, *even though Harold Woo probably wasn't poisoned, I STILL think this could be a murder mystery. So be careful.*

Frog signed the letter *K* with both hands. She tapped her right pinky finger on top of her left index finger twice, palms facing inward toward each other. "*Careful.*"

Charlie copied the sign, and then asked: *Careful about what?*

*Dex and Ray. And this guy Tony. That's the second time his name has been mentioned. So be careful. We don't even know what he looks like. He could be anyone.*

*So how can I be careful!?*

*Just have your key ready,* Frog wrote.

Although Charlie did plan to have his key ready, he did not want to be *told* to have his key ready. It made Dex and Ray—and Tony—that much scarier.

*I'll send you a letter*, Frog wrote, *about the next step of our investigation.*

*A letter?! That'll take days!*

*Not with him.* Frog gestured to Mr. Simple, who was coming out of the gondola station to unload passengers.

*Okay*, Charlie agreed. *And I have something I have to do anyway—with my grandparents.*

Mr. Simple helped shaky riders to the ground. He signed something to Frog, who was first in line to board. Frog signed back. Mr. Simple took a dollar from Frog and signed some more. As Frog boarded she gestured for Charlie to pay attention to Mr. Simple.

"I was just saying they're starting early," Mr. Simple said. "Frog here wanted to know what I meant. Those alumni folks, I said. Some of them are already here, riding the gondola over. I helped a little lady yesterday."

"Did she have a mole on her cheek?" Charlie asked.

*"That!"* Mr. Simple signed. That's who I mean.

Frog signed through the window. *"Aggie!"*

*"Alive!"* Charlie added, happy he knew that sign.

Mr. Simple collected more dollars. "Lots of former students go visit the grave of that author Frog loves. Pay their respects every year." Mr. Simple closed the gondola door.

*"I'll write you!"* Frog signed to Charlie through the window.

Mr. Simple entered the gondola station and pulled a lever. The gondola lurched ahead. Frog grinned. The other passengers did not.

• • •

Grandma Tickler held a jar of jelly beans in her lap, eating them one by one. Whenever Grandma Tickler found a black jelly bean she handed it to Grandpa Tickler, who popped it into his mouth.

Charlie's parents would be back in seventeen days.

In seventeen days he would be going to boarding school. Once he was there he would be gone for good. Perhaps Charlie wouldn't even get to go home for Christmas or summer vacation. His parents would enjoy having him gone so much that they would want him to stay there all the time. He would be forgotten.

Nobody would miss Charlie Tickler.

Charlie waited for a commercial. Then he stood in front of the television and turned down the volume.

"We can't see the television, Charlie," Grandma Tickler said. "We like the commercials, too, you know."

"Grandma, I want to do something together," Charlie said. "Something besides watching television."

"Besides television?" Grandma Tickler said. "Like what?"

Charlie held up a book. He had decided to read *Dorrie McCann and the Mystery of the Secret Treasure* instead of *Great Expectations*. In Charlie's opinion, Charles Dickens used way too many words—many of which Charlie didn't know. Chief Paley would love that book.

"Charlie wants to read to us, Irving!" Grandma Tickler shouted. "He wants to read us a book!"

"Ayuh," Grandpa Tickler said.

"No," Charlie said. "I want *you* to read to *me*. That's what grandparents *do*. They read to their grandchildren."

"I suppose," Grandma Tickler said, "if you sat in the front of the television set, we could watch you instead."

Charlie tried again. "It's the grandparents who are supposed to do the reading—"

"You'll have to read loud," Grandma Tickler said, leaning back in her E-Z chair recliner, "so Irving can hear."

Charlie sighed. Yvette peered around the corner, shook her head, and went back into the kitchen. Charlie turned off the television. His grandparents waited for the reading show to start.

Charlie held up the book, moving it in an arc so each viewer in his or her E-Z chair recliner could see. "*Dorrie McCann and the Mystery of the Secret Treasure*, by D. J. McKinnon."

"Dorrie McCann?" Grandma Tickler asked. "Irving, isn't that a movie?"

"Ayuh," Grandpa Tickler said.

"Charlie, there's a movie we can watch instead," Grandma Tickler said.

"There isn't a movie, Grandma," Charlie said.

"Are you sure?"

Charlie ignored this and started reading.

*"All her life—which wasn't that long, but still—people had said no to Dorrie McCann. It was always 'No, Dorrie,' or 'You can't do that, Dorrie,' or 'You might get hurt, Dorrie,' or 'You have to be able to hear to do that, Dorrie.' But Dorrie McCann never listened—not when she really wanted something."*

"That girl has a problem," Grandma Tickler said. "A problem with listening. When I say no to Irving, he listens to me."

"Ayuh!"

"You do listen, Irving—stop saying you don't!"

Charlie kept reading. *"Just today, in fact, Dorrie McCann had been told no. But Dorrie McCann's detective intuition told her something was not right. And Dorrie McCann always listened to her detective intuition."*

"Poppycock," Grandma Tickler interrupted again.

Charlie looked up. "What?"

"Detective intuition? Poppycock! I never heard of such a thing!"

"Ayuh," Grandpa Tickler said.

"It is not a real thing, Irving!" Grandma Tickler said.

Charlie thought about what his teacher would have said last year while reading a book to his class. "Grandma, would you mind holding your comments until the end of the chapter? Then we can discuss it."

"I suppose," Grandma Tickler grumbled.

Charlie continued with the story. Dorrie's favorite author had gone missing. She had left a note, however, just before she disappeared. Dorrie was certain the note contained a secret message—but she hadn't been able to find it. Dorrie's best friend, Jack, urged her to keep trying.

"*'I don't know if I can,' Dorrie told Jack. Her signing was small and unsure. She looked down at the note and shook her head.*

"*'You have to,' Jack signed. 'Remember, Deaf can!'*

"*'Why is it always Deaf can? Why not hearing can?'*

"*'Come on, Dorrie,' Jack begged. 'You know I'm lousy at solving ciphers.'*

"*Dorrie nodded. Jack was right. It was up to her. She reached into her top dresser drawer and pulled out a long red scarf. Dorrie wrapped the scarf around her neck and took a deep breath.*

"*'What are you doing?' Jack asked. 'It's hot in here.'*

"*'This isn't a scarf to keep you warm,' Dorrie said. 'It's a scarf to remember. My grandmother knitted it for my mother. She wanted Mom to always remember she had power inside of her.'*"

Charlie turned the page and paused. He looked

up from *Dorrie McCann and the Mystery of the Secret Treasure.*

Both of his grandparents were sound asleep, softly snoring in their E-Z chair recliners.

Yvette came into the living room. She put her fists on her hips. "Now I've got to wake them up before I leave or they'll sleep here all night."

"They weren't *supposed* to fall asleep," Charlie said. "They were *supposed* to stay awake and be interested."

"If it isn't on a screen, they aren't interested," Yvette said.

"There has to be something they like besides television," Charlie said.

"Sure there is," Yvette said. "It's called bed. Now help me wake them up so they can get into theirs."

# 17. Power

"Charlie!" Grandma Tickler called from downstairs. "Charlie, wake up! Walter Simple is here for you."

Charlie rolled out of bed. He picked up *Dorrie McCann and the Mystery of the Secret Treasure* from the floor. He had continued reading the book on his own last night. Charlie didn't remember much about what he had read before falling asleep except for one thing: Dorrie was just as determined as Frog.

Charlie rubbed the sleep from his eyes, pulled on shorts and a T-shirt, and went downstairs. Mr. Simple was on the front porch.

"Letter for Charlie Tickler," Mr. Simple said. He pulled a letter from his US Mail bag.

"That's me," Charlie said. He reached for the letter. Mr. Simple took a step back and held the letter close to his chest.

"Beautiful day out, wouldn't you say?" Mr. Simple gazed around the Ticklers' yard.

"I guess," Charlie said.

Yvette pulled Charlie inside. "He's waiting for a tip," she whispered. "That's why he didn't give it to your grandma. Irma's not a tipper."

"We have to tip the postman if we want our mail?" Charlie whispered back. "Is that legal?"

"Walter Simple doesn't work for the United States Post Office. He won that mailbag in a poker game."

"Oh," Charlie said. All the change Nate had given him from his hundred-dollar bill was upstairs.

Yvette saw him hesitate and said, "I'll go get my purse."

"Thank you, Yvette, but I have money. I'll be right back, Mr. Simple," Charlie called.

Mr. Simple beamed. "I'll wait."

• • •

Charlie tried giving Mr. Simple one dollar, but he did not look pleased. When Charlie gave him a second dollar Mr. Simple handed the letter over with a flourish.

> *Dear Charlie!*
> *I have to work until 4 p.m. today. Can you come for a sleepover after that? You can sleep in Oliver's bunk bed! Do you think your grandparents will let you? That will give us more time to investigate now that we know Aggie came here!!!*
> *Yours sincerely,*
> *Frog Castle*

Let him? Charlie could probably just go and his grandparents wouldn't notice he was gone unless he turned up on the television as a missing kid.

*That* they would notice.

The sound of a television news program blared from the living room. Charlie waited for a commercial.

Charlie asked.

"Ayuh?" Grandpa Tickler cupped his ear.

"Not sweet clover, Irving. Sleep over!" Grandma Tickler shouted. "We have a doctor's appointment today, you know," Grandma Tickler told Charlie. "Irving and I have bunions—both of us on both feet!"

"The sleepover, Grandma?" Charlie said. "It's at Frog's house, which is in Castle School for the Deaf. Can I go?"

"Ayuh." Grandpa Tickler nodded.

"If Irving says it's fine I suppose it's fine with me, too," Grandma Tickler said. "Just make sure to take your key. Remember, Charlie"—Grandma Tickler settled back into her recliner—"criminals are everywhere."

• • •

Charlie said a careful "Good morning" to the cat when he entered the library. Mr. Dickens eyed Charlie with pity. Charlie handed Miss Tweedy *Great Expectations*.

"My grandparents don't like books," Charlie said.

"Impossible," Miss Tweedy said. "Everyone loves books and everyone loves Charles Dickens. Perhaps you should try *Oliver Twist*?"

"What else did your grandparents do with you," Charlie asked, "besides reading?"

"Well, my grandmother was the most marvelous baker. Some of my fondest memories are with her in the kitchen, baking cookies and cakes."

Grandma and Grandpa Tickler did love to watch baking shows.

"Where are the baking books?" Charlie asked.

Miss Tweedy peered down at him over her pointy glasses. "The Dewey decimal system," she said. "Please tell me you've heard of it?"

"I think so—"

"The Dewey decimal system is a library classification system created by Melvil Dewey in 1876. Books are categorized into ten main classes. The Dewey decimal system is how this library maintains its pristine orderliness."

Charlie looked around at the dusty books piled on the floor, on the tables, and in overflowing bookshelves.

"Got it," he said.

"That is a card catalog." Miss Tweedy pointed to a wooden chest with many small drawers. "Once you find the book you will find its Dewey decimal number—a number"—Miss Tweedy picked up her thwacker and inkpad—"with a decimal point."

"Don't you have a computer I can use instead?" Charlie asked. "To find the book?"

Miss Tweedy peered down at Charlie over her pointy glasses. Again.

"The card catalog is a perfectly fine way for people to find books. Besides, in this village, computers are much too slow. Finding a card with your hands will be faster."

Charlie did not know the title of the book he was looking for, but it seemed unwise to say this out loud. He opened one wooden drawer with the letters *Ba–Bh* on it. The drawer was filled with cards, each with a book and its information. Charlie flipped through them, searching for book titles beginning with the word "bake." There was a basket with pencils and scrap paper on top of the card catalog. One book sounded just right. Charlie jotted down its Dewey decimal number (641.815) and showed the scrap of paper to Miss Tweedy.

"Ah. The six forties. Home and family management. Those books are kept by the potted fern."

Charlie looked through the stacks of books by the potted fern until he found the book with the Dewey decimal number 641.815: *Baking with the Grandkids: 101 Easy Recipes to Fill Their Stomachs and Your Heart.*

On the front was a picture of a plump grandma with rosy cheeks. She wore an apron and smiled sweetly at a boy eating a cupcake. There was no television anywhere near them.

• • •

Charlie had time before he had to meet Frog. He decided to stop at the police station and see if Chief Paley had found out anything about Aggie or Dex and Ray. But first he had an errand to do.

Charlie gripped his key between his knuckles, glad there were lots of people around. As he passed Junk and Stuff, his palms grew sweaty. The clerk was behind the counter, playing the guitar. Today he wasn't singing and he didn't have headphones on. Charlie stood outside and listened.

The clerk played as bad as he sang.

Charlie continued walking. At the stationery shop, Cartwright and Co., he bought a small notebook, the kind Frog used to write back and forth with hearing people. And a new pen. It didn't seem fair that Frog always had to use her notepad and pen to communicate.

As Charlie left the shop, he noticed the ivy-covered cottage with the purple front door. Charlie crossed the street.

### DESDEMONA FINKELSTEIN, F.T.E.

#### CASH ONLY

#### OPEN 10-4

#### (UNLESS THE UNIVERSE TELLS ME DIFFERENTLY)

What had Frog said?

Desdemona might have vital information for them.

Maybe he should wait for Frog. On the other hand, Dex and Ray were out there somewhere, looking for Aggie. The vital information from Desdemona Finkelstein, F.T.E., might just be what Charlie and Frog needed to find Aggie first.

Last time the door had been locked. Had the universe

told Desdemona to come to work today? Charlie reached for the brass doorknob and turned it.

It had.

• • •

A woman with short brown hair stood in the center of the cottage, as if waiting for Charlie.

"You came!" she said. "I knew you would!"

"Hi," Charlie said. "My name is—"

"Angus." The woman gave a wise nod.

"What?" Charlie said.

"Your name is Angus." She extended her hand. "Angus, it's a pleasure to meet—"

"No," Charlie said. "My name is—"

"Barry. Barry, it's a pleasure to meet—"

"Charlie," Charlie said. "My name is Charlie."

"That's what I was going to say next. It's a pleasure to meet you, Charlie. My name is Desdemona. Please have a seat."

Desdemona pointed to a chair in front of a desk. She moved behind the desk and sat. Rows of law books lined the bookshelves. Stacks of files were piled everywhere. Charlie brought his gaze back to Desdemona, who wore a navy blue suit.

"If I look like a lawyer," Desdemona said, "it's because I am one—was one—sort of still am one," she amended hastily. "I'm trying to transition to a new career. My parents insisted I study law, so I did. But it wasn't what *I* wanted." Desdemona leaned back, clasped her hands, and placed them on her desk. "But enough about me. The clock is ticking. I bill by the quarter hour. How can I help you?"

"I'm not sure," Charlie said. "My friend Frog said you might be able to help—"

"Frog? I love Frog! She taught me the best sign." Desdemona signed the letter *C* with one hand, and placed her fingertips and thumb on her opposite arm. *"Power."*

Charlie copied the sign. *"Power."*

"Power," Desdemona said. "We all have our own power."

"Okay," Charlie said. "Well, Frog said you might be able to give us some information."

"Charlie." Desdemona gave him a reproachful look. "I can't 'give'"—Desdemona made air quotes—"anyone anything. All I can do is bring out what's inside you."

"What exactly," Charlie asked, "is your new career?"

Desdemona pointed to a framed certificate on the wall.

DESDEMONA FINKELSTEIN IS HEREBY KNOWN AS A
FORTUNE-TELLER EXTRAORDINAIRE
UNLESS THE UNIVERSE TELLS HER DIFFERENTLY.
SIGNED,
DESDEMONA FINKELSTEIN, F.T.E.

"A fortune-teller?" Charlie said.

"Extraordinaire," Desdemona said.

Charlie stood up. "I think there's been a mistake—"

"SIT DOWN!" Desdemona was suddenly very lawyer-like.

Charlie sat.

Desdemona looked at him hard. "The universe brought you here for a reason, Charlie. Don't you want to know what that reason is?"

Before Charlie could answer, Desdemona said, "Give me your palm."

Charlie stretched out his left hand. Desdemona grabbed it and peered into it.

"I see a girl," she said. "She's Deaf."

"I just told you that," Charlie said. "It's Frog."

"I'm warming up," Desdemona said. She leaned forward again.

"I see a friendship forming between—nope, not a friendship. I see you and Frog *working together* to solve some sort of problem or puzzle or mystery."

"And then we become friends," Charlie said. "Right?"

"The line on your palm ends here, right after the mystery-puzzle-problem thing is solved. After that, I can't see what happens."

"But am I going to stay?" Charlie asked.

Desdemona looked up. "What's that?"

"Am I going to stay here? In Castle-on-the-Hudson."

"Well," Desdemona said, "that question, like the law, depends on how you interpret it. But I do have something for specific questions! My niece received two of these on her birthday, so she gave me one."

Desdemona reached under her desk and pulled out a Magic Black Ball.

Charlie gave Desdemona Frog's best are-you-kidding-me look.

"No," Desdemona said, "I am not kidding you. Any object can be powerful. But an object only gains power from those who believe. Not those who doubt. Now. Do you have questions or not? This baby has nineteen possible answers for you."

Charlie did have questions. Lots of them.

"Great." Desdemona pulled out a form. "Do you mind signing this contract for services rendered? It says the usual stuff—the fortune-teller isn't responsible for any actions you take because of the fortune told, nor is she responsible for damages, et cetera, et cetera."

Charlie signed his name, thinking Frog would never have signed anything without reading it carefully first. He picked up the Magic Black Ball.

He asked his first question. "Am I going to stay in Castle-on-the-Hudson?"

He turned over the ball.

*Anything is possible.*

Well, that was true. And as long as it was possible, it meant it could happen. Charlie closed his eyes again. Frog had said they needed to go to Desdemona for vital information. He thought about the most vital information he wanted to know.

"Is Aggie going to be all right?"

He opened his eyes and turned the ball over.

*No idea.*

"You have one more question," Desdemona whispered. "Then I have to bill you for the next quarter hour."

Charlie closed his eyes and took a deep breath. Maybe the ball knew the answer even if Desdemona didn't.

"Will Frog and I become friends?"

Charlie repeated the question to make sure the Magic Black Ball had heard him clearly.

He gave the ball a little shake and turned it over.

*Perhaps . . . perhaps not.*

• • •

Charlie left Desdemona Finkelstein, F.T.E., ten dollars lighter. He was tucking the rest of his money into his pocket when he walked right into two men.

Charlie looked up and stared into Dex's cold eyes.

"Hello," Ray said.

Charlie ran.

# 18. WWVVODMD?

Charlie didn't look back. He ran as fast as he could to the Castle-on-the-Hudson police station. Once again Chief Paley was on the phone, her feet propped up on her desk.

"Chief, I need to talk to you," Charlie gasped.

Chief Paley held up a finger.

"Yes, ma'am, I do understand," the chief said into the phone. "Yes, ma'am, you're making perfect sense. However, I'm feeling"—the chief reached for her word list—"denigrated as we converse. That means I am not feeling great while we're talking."

Silence. Listening.

"Yes, ma'am, I know you don't care. But is that a kind way to talk— Hello? Ma'am?"

Chief Paley sighed and hung up the phone.

Charlie jumped in. "Chief, I have to tell you—"

Chief Paley held up a hand. "Charlie, a writer's words are her tools. Do you know what I want to build with my tools?"

"Build?"

"It's a metaphor. Build with my tools, write with my words? A metaphor is a kind of cipher—a secret hidden in the words."

"I don't understand," Charlie said.

"I'll translate. Do you know what kind of books I want to write?"

"No," Charlie said. "But—"

"That was a rhetorical question. That means I don't expect an answer because I already know the answer. Mysteries. I plan to write mystery books set in a village on the Hudson River with a brave and brilliant chief of police. It's a quiet little village, but it's those quiet little villages that have the most secrets. And where there are secrets"—Chief Paley lowered her voice to a whisper—"there is crime."

"Crime!" Charlie said. "That's why I'm here."

"Crime? Why didn't you say so?"

"I tried—never mind," Charlie said. "I just saw Dex and Ray. The men looking for Aggie!"

"What were they doing?" the chief asked. "I never found them yesterday."

"Well," Charlie said, "they were just standing on the sidewalk. Ray said hello."

"That was friendly of him," Chief Paley said.

"Not really," Charlie said. He told the chief about Dex and Ray following him and Frog into Junk and Stuff.

"But has a crime been committed?" Chief Paley said. "To answer that question I always follow the WWVVODMD rule. I'm sure you're familiar with it."

"Um, no," Charlie said.

"What Would Vince Vinelli or Dorrie McCann Do?"

Charlie's left hand repeated the letters. WWVVODMD.

Chief Paley looked at Vince Vinelli's picture. "Vince Vinelli would say good people have to do something if a crime has been committed. Dorrie McCann would use her detective intuition and investigate any possible criminal activity. So let's take another look-see around the village and find these men. But tell me something, Charlie Tickler." The chief drummed her fingers on the desk. "Why do you care so much about this Aggie? You don't even know her." She leaned back in her chair and waited for Charlie's response.

"Why do I care?" Charlie had not really thought about it. Parents, giant golden moles, boarding school, grandparents, and E-Z chair recliners flashed through his mind.

Suddenly the reason was simple and clear.

"I care," Charlie said, "because everyone needs someone who cares about them. And I don't know if anyone else cares about Aggie."

• • •

Chief Paley hung a Back Soon! sign on the front door of the police department. Together she and Charlie searched Castle-on-the-Hudson. Charlie felt very small and very safe next to Chief Paley. But Dex and Ray were nowhere to be found.

"Charlie, I have to get back to the station. You see those two men again you come get me pronto." The chief gave Charlie a bone-jarring pat on the back before striding away.

Without the chief next to him, Charlie did not feel so safe anymore. Charlie spotted Herman and his taxi waiting at the red light. In the backseat were Grandma and Grandpa Tickler, heading home from their bunion appointment.

"Grandma!" Charlie knocked on her window. Grandma Tickler rolled it down.

"Can I ride home with you?" Charlie asked. The

light turned green. The taxi began to roll away. Charlie jogged along beside it.

"Herman never stops for other fares until he gets to his destination," Grandma Tickler said. Both of Herman's hands clutched the steering wheel with his chin resting on top of them. "But," Grandma Tickler suggested, "you could just jump into the front seat."

Charlie grabbed the front door handle, yanked it open, and jumped in.

Herman didn't even glance over.

# 19. Mom and Dad

Charlie was eating a bologna sandwich, looking through *Baking with the Grandkids: 101 Easy Recipes to Fill Their Stomachs and Your Heart*, when the phone rang.

"Tickler residence. Charlie speaking."

The phone had a long, curly cord. Charlie could walk back to the kitchen table and still talk.

"Charlie?" said a faraway voice.

"Dad!"

Loud crackling filled Charlie's ear.

"Darling? Can you hear us?" Charlie's mother was also on the phone.

"Mom! I can hear you!" Charlie said.

"Can you hear anything, Alistair?" his mother asked his father.

"Charlie? We made it to South Africa!" Charlie's father said. "The giant golden moles are most appreciative that we're helping them and— Myra, I don't think he can hear me."

"I can hear you! Can you hear me?" Charlie shouted into the phone.

Yvette came up from the basement with a laundry basket. "I sure can hear you," she said before heading upstairs.

"Darling, we're having the most marvelous time. The weather has been perfect. We have been swimming every day. Your father is so glad he brought two swim-suits, aren't you, Alistair?"

"That was good packing advice, Myra."

"Charlie? Darling? Are you there?"

"I'm here!" Charlie said. "I'm here!"

Charlie opened the kitchen door and went out on the steps, stretching the curly cord until it was straight.

"Mom! Dad! Can you hear me now?"

"I don't hear Charlie," his father said to his mother. "The connection is too weak."

And no matter how loud Charlie shouted, no matter

how clearly he could hear his parents, they could not hear him. His parents hung up. Charlie went back to the wall and put the phone on the hook.

Yvette came back downstairs with the laundry basket filled with towels and sheets.

"Well?" she asked.

"They couldn't hear me," Charlie said.

"The connection was just bad," Yvette said. "South Africa is a long way off."

"I could hear them." Charlie pushed his plate away.

"Well, sometimes the connection's better on one end," Yvette said.

Charlie didn't respond.

Yvette started to say something else and stopped. She sighed and went down to the basement to start a load of laundry.

Charlie practiced the signs Millie had shown him. "*Mom*"—the thumb of his open hand touched his chin—and "*Dad*"—the thumb of his open hand touched his forehead. *"Mom and Dad."*

He looked in the living room. Charlie's grandparents were napping in their E-Z chair recliners, plates of pimento-and-cheese sandwiches still on their laps. He returned to the baking book, more determined than ever to find something so delicious to bake with his grandparents that they would want to make it again and again. With Charlie.

# 20. Frog

The gondola swung in the gusty wind. Charlie breathed a sigh of relief when the cabin swept its way to the top of the bluff. Oliver opened the door and placed a stool underneath it.

"The gondola," Oliver whispered to Charlie as he stepped out, "isn't supposed to operate in wind like this."

But Oliver hadn't whispered softly enough. The woman behind Charlie gasped.

"It's perfectly safe," Oliver assured her with a brilliant smile. "Would this face lie?" Oliver moved closer to Charlie. "Wait for me while I tell Mr. Simple to ixnay ethay ondolagay until the storm blows over."

Ixnay ethay ondolagay?

"Nix the gondola? Pig Latin? It's a kind of cipher?" Oliver shook his head at Charlie's confused look. "What do they teach kids these days?"

Once Oliver had radioed Mr. Simple, he and Charlie leaned into the wind and walked up to the castle. Charlie dropped off his backpack in Oliver's room, and then they headed back down to the great hall.

"Just to warn you," Oliver said. "Mom always gets a bit . . . intense this time of year."

"Why?" Charlie asked.

"The Founders' Day Dinner. Every year she wants the castle to look perfect for the alumni. That means we all have to pitch in. Forced labor. Frog was only allowed to invite you over because she told Mom you're interested in the castle. It's your cover while you investigate your murder mystery."

"Not murder," Charlie said. "Just mystery."

"If that makes you feel better," Oliver said.

"It does," Charlie said.

"So what have you guys discovered so far about your not-murder-just-a-mystery?" Oliver asked.

"I'll tell you if you tell me what you did," Charlie said. "Frog told me you did something only she knows about. That's why you have to interpret for her."

"Wow." Oliver paused on the stone steps. "You're a lot smarter than you look, Charlie Tickler."

"Thanks," Charlie said. "I think."

Millie was skipping up the stairs with Bear at her heels.

"Hi, Millie," Charlie said.

"Hi, Charlie! I'm doing a special project," Millie told him. "It's a secret."

"Sure it is," Oliver said.

Millie stamped her foot. Bear growled. "It is, Oliver! You'll see! Bye, Charlie." Millie continued up the steps.

"Bye, Millie." Oliver turned to Charlie. "Millie cannot keep a secret. Don't tell her anything unless you want everyone to know." Oliver pointed to a man entering the great hall. "There's my dad." The man paused and looked around carefully before hurrying toward them. Oliver signed to him. His father turned to Charlie and shook his hand.

"It's a pleasure to meet you, Charlie. I'm Henry Hollander. I always have to explain to people that I did not take the Castle family name, although my children did."

"Just call him Mr. Castle," Oliver said and signed. "Everyone does."

"Indeed! If it's easier to remember, then by all means do so!" Mr. Castle was hard of hearing, and although his voice sounded tinny and far away, Charlie could understand him perfectly. "Frog tells me you're interested in our school history. Why don't you come up to the superintendent's study with me before Frog gives you the tour? I'll give you a lengthy but, I assure you, not boring introduction."

"Dad is writing a history of our school," Oliver said and signed. "He's using Grandpa Sol's office while Grandpa's away. Dad, I'm sure Charlie would love to hear your lengthy, but definitely not boring, talk. Wouldn't you, Charlie?" Oliver grinned.

"Well," Charlie said, "I'm supposed to be meeting Frog—"

"Oh, you have plenty of time," Oliver said.

"Excellent!" Mr. Castle took Charlie's arm. "But let's hurry." His eyes darted around the great hall. "It's not good to stand where it's so open and unprotected. My wife is hunting for—I mean, looking for—people to help with her list of chores, and I would much rather not— Agh!" Mr. Castle dropped Charlie's arm.

Mrs. Castle stood at the top of the stone steps, arms crossed, foot tapping.

She signed something to Mr. Castle. Charlie turned to Oliver. But Oliver had disappeared. Mr. Castle signed back, pointing to Charlie and then toward upstairs. Mrs. Castle shook her head no. She looked at her list and pointed to the statue in the middle of the great hall.

Mr. Castle turned to Charlie. "My wife thinks it

would be better if we discussed history while we polished the Alice and Francine statue."

Mrs. Castle came down the steps and handed Mr. Castle a bottle of polish and rags. She checked something off her long list and marched back up the stairs.

"Eleanor," Mr. Castle told Charlie, "gets very anxious this time of year. Not only does she want the castle to look its best for returning students, but this time every year my father-in-law hikes to a special spot on the Appalachian Trail. It's the place where he proposed to his late wife. He always arrives the same day he proposed. Eleanor worries until he returns home."

Charlie and Mr. Castle stood next to the Alice and Francine statue in the middle of the great hall. Two girls faced each other smiling. The younger girl was making the letter *F* with one hand. The older girl was making the letter *A*. Between them sat a small frog with a satisfied look on its face. On the base of the statue was a plaque with one word: FRIENDS.

They would need a ladder to polish the whole statue. Charlie fingerspelled LADDER. Mr. Castle shrugged and put some polish on his cloth and on Charlie's. They began polishing the parts they could reach.

"Would you like to know why Francine is called Frog?" Mr. Castle asked Charlie. Charlie nodded. He would like to know. Mr. Castle patted the statue.

"The Alice and Francine statue holds the answer.

Over two hundred years ago, the first Francine Castle was born deaf. Her parents, who were hearing, didn't know how to educate her much less talk with her. Then they visited a school for Deaf children, and met a Deaf girl named Alice."

As Charlie polished and listened, he spotted Millie at the top of the staircase. She held a brown paper bag filled with something. Millie continued with Bear down the hall, away from the Castle family apartment.

"When Francine and her parents arrived at the Deaf school," Mr. Castle continued, "they found Alice sitting outside, scrutinizing a large frog. Little Francine ran over to look. The frog leaped. Alice signed 'frog,' and pointed to it. Francine pointed to the frog and repeated the sign. She then began hopping around like a frog herself. Francine's parents were amazed! Francine had understood immediately what that sign meant. Today, Charlie, this is how we sign 'frog' in American Sign Language, or ASL."

Mr. Castle placed a fist, palm down, under his chin. He flicked his index and middle finger out in a *V* shape twice. "*Frog.*" Charlie copied the sign.

"When our Francine heard the story of her name-sake, she loved it so much she insisted she was to be called Frog. She must have been about three years old. Or was she four?"

A hand with a jewel-studded bracelet on its wrist

tapped Mr. Castle on the shoulder. Mr. Castle signed to Frog.

"*Three,*" Frog answered.

"I was just telling Charlie the story of your name," Mr. Castle signed and spoke. "Yes, I know you want to start your tour. Yes, I realize you must hurry before your mother has you doing chores. I'm almost finished. Now, where was I?"

Charlie fingerspelled ALICE.

"Ah, yes. Alice. Alice stayed for several weeks, teaching sign language to Francine. It was then that Francine's father decided his home, this castle, would become a school for Deaf children. Rooms were made into classrooms. Dorms were built for students to sleep in."

"You mean it was a boarding school?" Charlie fingerspelled BOARDING SCHOOL in case Mr. Castle didn't understand him.

"Indeed it was and still is," Mr. Castle replied. "Children go home on the weekends if their parents live close by. But many students return to their families only for the holidays and spring and summer break. The school, you see, becomes their home."

Charlie thought about finding a new home at the faraway boarding school where his parents were planning to send him. He thought about wanting his parents to be as interested in him as they were in northern hairynosed wombats.

Frog tugged on Charlie's arm.

"But we didn't finish." Charlie gestured to the statue with his rag.

"Nothing is ever really finished, is it, Charlie?" Mr. Castle said. "You have a tour to take and I have some reading to do. Let's both hurry before my wife catches us."

# 21. Graveyard

A peacock wandered the castle grounds. He squawked and spread his tail feathers at the sight of Charlie and Frog. Charlie watched him shimmy and shake around the yard.

Frog started to pull out her notebook, but Charlie was faster. The pages of his new notebook fluttered in the wind. Charlie held them down as he wrote with his new pen: *Now you don't have to use up all your paper and ink,* he explained.

Frog took Charlie's pen. Underneath his sentence she drew a smiley face. With an exclamation point.

Then Frog wrote: *We know Aggie came to the castle. But WHY?*

*To get away from Dex and Ray?* Charlie suggested.

*To look for the secret?* Frog wondered.

*Or both?* Charlie wrote.

Thick black clouds hung overhead. The wind carried the scent of fresh-cut grass and the salty smell of the Hudson River. Frog's hair blew in her face. She pushed it away with an impatient hand.

*If the secret is a book,* Frog wrote, *then Aggie might have tried the school library. We can investigate there after dinner. Maybe something's hidden inside a book! Or maybe there's a cipher in a book. Both a secret treasure and a hidden code were in Dorrie McCann's first mystery!*

*Maybe,* Charlie wrote.

*Maybe is all we have,* Frog replied.

Thunder echoed in the distance.

*We shouldn't be outside in a thunderstorm,* Charlie wrote. *My grandparents' TV antenna got struck by lightning during the last one.*

Frog waved this information away and kept writing. *Aggie signed "dead" to you. I think that's a clue about where we need to go next.*

Frog paused, pen in the air. Her jeweled bracelet slid down her arm. When she was certain she had Charlie's attention she wrote: *The graveyard.*

Frog curved both her hands, palms facing down,

and then she arced her hands back toward her body. *"Graveyard."*

Charlie couldn't help signing it even though he didn't want to.

• • •

Several large stone buildings ringed the castle. DORMS, Frog spelled. The wooden doors were locked for the summer. They tugged on the handle of each door—just in case.

Charlie and Frog circled behind the castle and came to a stone barn. A horse and a cow munched hay while three chickens wandered, clucking at one another. A man was mucking out a stall.

*That's Obie,* Frog wrote. *He's the castle caretaker. He NEVER goes into the graveyard.*

Before Charlie could ask why, Frog went to the stall Obie was cleaning. She banged on it. Obie lifted his head and spun around. His eyes were milky blue.

Obie was Deaf *and* blind.

Frog touched his arm. Obie put out his hands. Frog put her hands under his and signed. How did Obie do that? Understand Frog just with his hands and not his eyes?

Frog motioned for Charlie to come over. She gestured for Charlie to fingerspell his name.

Obie put his hand on top of Charlie's hand, his fingers feeling the letters Charlie formed. Obie had wild, white hair with eyebrows just as wild and white. CHARLIE, Obie spelled back Charlie's name.

Charlie nodded, then remembered Obie couldn't see him. Charlie signed *"yes,"* nodding his fist up and down. Obie pointed to Frog, who was standing next to him with her hand on his shoulder. Obie fingerspelled BEHAVE? His bushy eyebrows lifted upward.

Was Frog behaving?

Frog made a face. Charlie signed *"yes,"* even though he was probably telling a lie.

Satisfied, Obie went back to cleaning the stalls.

Charlie pulled out his notebook. *Why doesn't Obie go into the graveyard?*

*He says it's haunted.*

*Haunted?*

*Silly, right?*

A chill swept up Charlie's spine.

Three goats grazed outside the barn. The largest one bleated as more thunder rumbled. Charlie and Frog continued toward the graveyard. A stone wall ran behind the goats and the barn. Charlie's fingers traced the rough stones as he and Frog walked beside it. Frog stopped at an old wooden door set in the wall.

She turned the handle. The door opened with a loud *creeeeeaaak*.

Charlie peered over her shoulder as he stepped through the doorway behind her.

Moss-covered headstones tilted at awkward angles under trees. A small stone church sat on the right. Under the darkening sky the graveyard was eerie. And definitely, Charlie decided, haunted.

*If Obie won't go in*, Charlie wrote, *maybe we shouldn't go in, either.*

Frog snorted and moved deeper into the graveyard.

Charlie sighed and followed. He tried stepping lightly on the ground. The trees in the graveyard rustled and swayed. The thunder grew louder and closer. Charlie scanned the sky. They shouldn't be under trees. He distracted himself by reading the inscriptions on the headstones.

HERE LIES THE BODY OF

OTIS T. JENKINS

1845–1896

I TOLD YOU I WAS SICK!


HERE LIES THE BODY OF

BERNADETTE MILLS

1835–1899

I TOLD YOU, TOO!

BUT YOU WOULD NOT LISTEN!

HERE LIES THE BODY OF

EDWARD HYDE

1816–1909

NO ONE EVER LISTENS (SIGH),

UNTIL IT IS TOO LATE.

And then there was this one:

HERE LIES THE BODY OF

HORACE T. BELLOWS

1875–1949

HE COULDN'T HEAR,

BUT HE LISTENED WITH HIS HEART.

He couldn't hear, but he listened with his heart.

Frog listened with her eyes.

Obie listened with his hands.

And anyone, if they really wanted to, could listen with their heart.

But how could you make people listen when they are too far away to hear you?

First, they had to *want* to listen.

Frog tapped Charlie on the shoulder.

*"What's wrong?"* she signed.

What's wrong was that Charlie wanted to stay in Castle-on-the-Hudson.

He wanted to keep learning sign language.

He wanted to be friends with Frog.

Charlie and Frog sat down next to Horace T. Bellows.

Charlie told Frog about his parents and how they loved helping—animals, that is. How they were in South Africa helping giant golden moles, but would soon be back to take Charlie to a faraway boarding school. So they could help animals without also having to help Charlie.

Charlie sighed. *My parents care a lot about animals. Just not about me.*

*They have to care!* Frog wrote. *That's what it means to be a family—you have to care!*

Charlie shrugged.

*You should tell them,* Frog wrote.

*I try to talk to them. They don't hear me.*

*Lots of people don't hear me. So I MAKE them listen.*

*How?*

*I communicate in any way possible. And I don't stop until I get what I want!*

Charlie thought about that. Then he wrote: *Your dad said students call Castle School for the Deaf their home. So maybe the boarding school will one day feel like home. Maybe I will like it—I should have asked the Magic Black Ball if I was going to like it.*

*You went to see Desdemona?!*

Charlie nodded. *I thought she could help us find Aggie. But she didn't have any vital information.*

*The vital information is inside us! Desdemona just helps bring it out.*

*With a Magic Black Ball?* Charlie asked.

*The ball is just something to help. It's the person who has the power.*

Another rumble overhead. Charlie plucked a piece of grass and pulled his knees up to his chin. A crow cawed. Another crow answered.

Frog tapped his shoulder. She showed him her notebook.

*Come on. I'm going to show you my favorite grave here. It's in the back.*

Frog stood. She stuck out her hand and pulled Charlie to his feet. Charlie followed Frog on the winding path to the grave of D. J. McKinnon, author of the Dorrie McCann books.

The wind gusted. A small white paper fluttered by. Frog grabbed it.

It was a gum wrapper. A sugar-free cinnamon gum wrapper.

Dex and Ray.

Charlie and Frog looked around. Dex and Ray were here. Or—Charlie and Frog moved closer together—Dex and Ray *are* here.

Thunder boomed.

Charlie made a we-have-to-go gesture.

A fork of lightning lit up the sky.

Charlie made a we-have-to-go-RIGHT-NOW gesture.

Thunder crashed. Rain poured down. Charlie and Frog raced back to the castle.

# 22. Home

Mrs. Castle piled lentils and peas onto Charlie's plate. He stared at the brown-green mush and remembered Yvette's meat loaf. He took a cautious bite, hoping for the best.

It was not the best.

Everyone else seemed to like the mush. They sat at the large round table, eating and signing while Charlie poked at his dinner. Occasionally Oliver would interpret, but mostly Charlie had no idea what was going on. Instead, he thought about all of his unanswered questions.

Dex and Ray had come to the castle. First and most

important question—were they still here? Second question—why had Dex and Ray come? To look for Aggie? To look for the same thing Aggie was looking for? Or both? Charlie swirled the mush into brown-green circles and brought his attention back to the conversation.

Mrs. Castle was signing. Her eyebrows, eyes, mouth, shoulders, arms, hands—all were part of what she was saying. Frog had the same expressions as her mother. Mr. Castle wasn't nearly as interesting to watch. His signs were much smaller than Mrs. Castle's and Frog's, and his face did not move as much. It was hard to watch Oliver sign as Charlie was sitting right next to him. Millie was busy feeding Bear under the table.

Smart Millie.

Mrs. Castle banged the table to get Millie's attention. Charlie didn't need an interpreter to tell him Mrs. Castle was saying, *"Millie! Stop feeding Bear your dinner."*

Mrs. Castle signed something else.

"Mom's telling Millie she's ruining her appetite with all those peanut-butter-and-jelly sandwiches she's been making," Oliver told Charlie.

"I am not ruining my appetite, Oliver!" Millie yelled.

"Don't blame the messenger, Millie," Oliver said. "I'm just telling Charlie what Mom said."

Mrs. Castle looked pointedly at Charlie's plate. She signed to him. It was clear what she was saying. Charlie ate another tiny bite of brown-green mush.

Mrs. Castle snorted.

Charlie took a much bigger bite.

Satisfied, Mrs. Castle began talking again.

*"So, Charlie, I know Frog has been teaching you signs,"* Mrs. Castle said as Oliver interpreted. *"But I hope Frog has explained that signs are only part of ASL—"*

*"Mom!"*

Mrs. Castle ignored Frog. *"Because how you move your face and how you move your body are also part of our language—"*

*"Mom! Charlie doesn't care—"*

*"—using signs while speaking English is a way to communicate; but it's not ASL, which Frog should be teaching you—"*

*"Mom! I am!"* Frog kicked Charlie under the table. Charlie nodded vigorously.

*"Good,"* Mrs. Castle said. *"That's important. So, Charlie, why did your family move to Castle-on-the-Hudson?"*

"It's just me," Charlie said. "Not my parents."

Mrs. Castle gave Charlie a sharp look. *"Why?"* she asked. *"Where are your parents?"*

"My parents are busy helping," Charlie explained. "Right now they're helping in South Africa."

*"Helping who?"*

"Giant golden moles," Charlie answered.

*"Moles need help?"*

"Giant golden moles do," Charlie said. "I guess."

"*For how long?*"

"Three weeks," Charlie said. "Well, now it's down to sixteen more days." Mrs. Castle's brow furrowed, so Charlie quickly added, "But I'm staying with my grandparents."

Mrs. Castle nodded approvingly. "*Good,*" she said again. "*Our own grandpa Sol will be back tonight. I'll be relieved when he's home. He still has to write his speech for the Founders' Day Dinner! And I still have my to-do list, which is growing longer by the minute.*" Mrs. Castle whipped out her long sheet of paper. "*I expect everyone to pitch in. I want this school cleaned from top to bottom. Frog, I want you and Charlie to clean the glass on the class-room doors after dinner. You don't mind helping, do you, Charlie?*"

Charlie gave Mrs. Castle a thumbs-up with one hand and drank water with the other. A brown-green blob was stuck in his throat.

Mrs. Castle shined a smile on Charlie and then turned it off to glare at Frog. "*I'm sure Charlie never makes rude faces when his mother asks him for help,*" she said. Oliver seemed to enjoy interpreting that.

• • •

Charlie and Frog sat at the top of the stone staircase. Rain lashed at the windowpanes. The castle felt dark and vast and empty. Or was it? Right now it seemed like a perfect place for criminals.

*We need to be careful*, Charlie wrote. *Dex and Ray could still be here.*

*Good! We can catch them!*

*Bad! We're just kids!*

*We'll be careful. Promise! We need to investigate the school library.*

*We need to clean the glass on the classroom doors.*

"*That*," Frog signed. That's what I mean.

Charlie wondered.

*Maybe*, Frog wrote, *there's a criminology section in our library—the same section Aggie went to in the village library.*

*Isn't your library for kids?*

*Kids are interested in criminology!*

Frog told Charlie the school library was locked during the summer because Mean Librarian, or ML as Frog liked to call her, didn't want anyone in the library when she wasn't there. Only ML and the superintendent had a key—which meant Frog's mother had a key, since Grandpa Sol wasn't home yet. And Frog's mother believed in following ML's rules since ML was, after all, the librarian.

*So how do we get in without a key?* Charlie asked.

*You'll see*, Frog answered.

Frog led Charlie down the hall away from the Castle

family apartment. She continued up another set of stairs. At the next landing she went down another corridor and up a narrow flight of steps. At the top was a short hallway that ended with an arched door. Frog went over to a painting of the Hudson River. One of the tugboats had a small handle. Frog moved it to the right. A panel slid open, revealing a secret space.

A perfect place to hide a key.

Except the hiding space was empty.

Frog turned to Charlie, puzzled. She looked on the floor. No key.

"What are you doing?" said a voice. Charlie jumped and knocked into Frog, who knocked into the painting.

It was Millie. And Bear.

"You scared me, Millie!" Charlie said.

Frog signed furiously to Millie, who signed back and then stomped away.

*I told her I was giving you a tour and to leave us alone! Oliver must have the key.*

*What about Millie?*

*Millie can't keep a secret. Only Oliver, James, and I know about the key.*

*Who's James?*

*My older brother. He's backpacking around the world. Now we have to wait to investigate the library.* Frog sighed. *I suppose we have to clean now.*

Frog led Charlie down to the great hall and past the half-polished statue of Alice and Francine. Shadows and dark corners gave criminals plenty of places to hide. And pounce.

Frog turned into a hall lined with classrooms. Charlie peered into the first one as lightning flashed outside the windows. A skeleton leered. Charlie stumbled backward. Frog laughed and fingerspelled SCIENCE CLASS.

Charlie had never heard Frog laugh out loud before. It was a rich, full-bellied laugh. Charlie liked hearing it.

*Oliver loves our science teacher*, Frog wrote. *I do, too! But my favorite teacher is my English teacher!*

*Oliver goes to school here?* Charlie asked. *But he's hearing!*

*He's a Castle! Castle children have gone to school here for generations—even if they are hearing! All Castle children are bilingual in ASL and English.*

Charlie took a cloth and a spray bottle. He began cleaning as he absorbed this new information. The classroom desks were set up in a U-shape, not in rows. It was, Charlie realized, so students could see one another. Frog obviously loved her school. And it really was her home.

Charlie had a thought. He stopped wiping the glass and took out his notebook.

*Maybe Aggie was just coming home. How do you sign "home"?*

Frog placed her thumb and fingertips together in a flattened O-shape. She touched them to the side of her chin and then moved them up to her cheek. Charlie copied her. "*Home.*"

*What do you mean?* Frog asked. *Just coming home?*

*Maybe Aggie was a student here once. So that would mean this was her other home—*

Frog dropped her rag. She slumped to the floor.

Charlie grabbed her shoulder. "Frog! What is it?"

Frog motioned limply for Charlie's pen and paper.

*I'm a HORRIBLE detective!* Frog wrote.

"*Why?*" Charlie signed.

*I missed something so OBVIOUS. What you said, about Aggie being a student. I don't deserve to be called detective!*

Frog threw the pen and paper down and covered her face with her hands.

Charlie awkwardly patted Frog on the back. He picked up the paper and pen from the floor and sat next to Frog. He wrote a note and tapped Frog's shoulder.

*Everyone makes mistakes, Frog. I bet even Dorrie McCann made mistakes!*

Frog gasped. Charlie could tell Frog was thinking, Dorrie McCann make a mistake? Impossible! In Charlie's mind's eye he signed *"impossible."*

But then Frog nodded.

*SEE?* Charlie wrote. *If Dorrie can make mistakes, so can you.*

Charlie stood. He reached out his hand. Frog took it and jumped to her feet. She led Charlie to a passageway on the other side of the great hall. These walls were lined with framed photographs of each year's graduating class.

Charlie had no idea how old Aggie was. They started with the oldest photograph at the end of the hallway. Charlie studied each one before moving on to the next.

1923 ... 1930 ... 1935 ... 1938 ... 1942 ... 1949 ... and on and on.

Until suddenly, there she was. First row. Bright eyes. Warm smile. A large mole was on her cheek.

Aggie.

# 23. Kiss-Fist

Mr. Castle was stretched out on the leather sofa, snoring in the superintendent's study. Books were shelved on floor-to-ceiling bookcases, with a rolling ladder to reach the highest ones.

Frog went over to a bookcase by the fireplace and crouched down. Charlie crouched beside her. There were dozens of Castle School for the Deaf yearbooks. Frog trailed her finger along the spines until she found Aggie's senior yearbook.

Frog flipped through pictures of the debate club, the drama club, the sports teams. She came to the graduating class, listed in alphabetical order. Charlie and Frog studied each name and picture. They read the few sentences below each one.

At the letter *C* Frog paused.

Frog's grandpa had Frog's big eyes. Or rather Frog had his big eyes. Underneath his picture it read:

**SOLOMON JAMES CASTLE**
Sol's favorite pastime is reading the
dictionary. He enjoys hiking and fishing,
and plans to be the next superintendent
of Castle School for the Deaf (of course!).

Frog turned more pages. She tapped on a picture of a young woman with pointy glasses like Miss Tweedy's.

**DOROTHY JANE McKINNON**
D.J. helps everyone see his or her own
power. A better writer and a better
human being cannot be found.

Frog gave a happy sigh and kissed the back of her fist. "*Kiss-fist.*"

Kiss-fist, Charlie realized, was used for anything Frog really loved—books, sparkly jewelry, coffee, Vince Vinelli. And of course Dorrie McCann and D. J. McKinnon. Frog loved a lot of things.

Frog continued to turn pages. Finally, there was Aggie.

### AGATHA E. PENDERWICK

Aggie is a loving friend but not a good
secret keeper!
She adores knitting and is always
making things for her friends.

Charlie and Frog stared at the young Aggie.

*Look at her eyes*, Charlie wrote. *She looks worried.*

Frog pointed to the words "not a good secret keeper."

*Aggie couldn't keep a secret—even back then!*

*Maybe that's why she looks worried*, Charlie replied.

Mr. Castle gave a loud snore and woke himself up. Charlie nudged Frog and pointed to the couch.

"Frog! I was just taking a short break from your mother's to-do list. Charlie, I'm delighted to see you're so interested in our school's history!" Mr. Castle spoke and signed at the same time. "What are you looking at?"

Frog held up the yearbook.

"Ah! Grandpa's class! And D. J. McKinnon's class! There is some intrigue with that year. I need to discuss it with Grandpa. Did you know the Appalachian Trail is over two thousand miles long, and extends from—"

Frog interrupted her father with a question, the same one Charlie had. She signed, *"What intrigue?"*

"What intrigue? Well . . ." Mr. Castle reached for

the bowl of pistachio nuts next to him. He cracked a nut and popped it in his mouth before he continued. Mr. Castle switched to ASL. He signed first and then spoke into English for what he had just signed.

*"There was some jealousy over D. J. McKinnon's success. Apparently she wrote the first draft of her Dorrie McCann series here, when she was a senior. Somehow a friend who was not really a friend found out about the manuscript. A frenemy is what Oliver calls it."*

Mr. Castle ate another pistachio.

Frog stamped her foot for Mr. Castle to finish.

*"It was widely rumored that D.J.'s frenemy burned the manuscript. Every last word of it."*

Frog gasped first. Then Charlie.

*"I know. Awful. There was no way to prove it, of course. Luckily D.J. remembered most of her story and rewrote it after she graduated. As you know she became a book printer and published the first Dorrie McCann books herself. Did you know Grandpa Sol has a copy of every book written by an alumnus?"* Mr. Castle pointed to the top of a bookshelf between two tall windows. *"Except, of course, the Dorrie McCann books. Grandpa Sol gave Frog those books."*

"Charlie," Mr. Castle now spoke and signed, "if you like yearbooks then you are going to find my own yearbook fascinating—"

But Frog was already pulling on Charlie's arm as she signed something to her father.

"Of course you must finish your cleaning," Mr. Castle agreed. "I should go help your mother as well. Charlie, my yearbook will have to wait."

Mr. Castle reached for another pistachio nut.

# 24. Scared

From the top bunk bed Charlie watched Oliver do push-ups in his pajamas.

"Eighteen ... nineteen ..."

Oliver lowered himself for number twenty. He stayed on the floor so long Charlie wondered if he was all right. Finally Oliver straightened his skinny arms.

"Twenty!" He flopped to the floor with a final grunt.

Oliver reached for his glasses. Then he picked up a book and crawled into the bottom bunk.

Oliver did not have the school library key. This was

Charlie's takeaway from the fight Frog and Oliver had right before bed. The missing school library key was now another puzzle to solve.

Charlie should have been reading *Dorrie McCann and the Mystery of the Secret Treasure.* Instead he reached for *Baking with the Grandkids: 101 Easy Recipes to Fill Their Stomachs and Your Heart.* Oliver was a really good baker. Charlie leaned over the bunk bed.

"Your cake was great."

"Thanks," Oliver said. "Mom always cooks dinner. I started baking so we'd have dessert to look forward to."

"Oliver, what's the most delicious thing to bake? Something that would make someone want you around forever—just so you could bake it again?"

"Hmmm. You're talking about Frog, I'm guessing?"

"No!" Charlie's face turned hot.

"Good, because that's kind of gross," Oliver said. "So how much baking have you done? My recipes have a definite hierarchy of complexities."

"None."

"None?" Oliver gave Charlie the Frog look. "Okay. Never baked before but want something guaranteed to make someone want more. Let me think." Oliver snapped his fingers. "Be right back."

Oliver left and came back a few minutes later. He handed Charlie a bag of chocolate chips.

"Chocolate chip cookies," Oliver said. "They smell

awesome when they're baking, they're easy to make, and everyone loves them. Recipe's on the back."

"Thanks, Oliver."

Charlie closed *Baking with the Grandkids*. He had his recipe.

"Mom will be here in a minute," Oliver said. "She insists on tucking me in. She'll tuck you in, too. Whoever sleeps over is one of her kids until the sleepover is done. She even tucks in my older brother. He's twenty!"

"Is your older brother Deaf or hearing?"

"James is Deaf. I think he's in Peru right now. He's missing Founders' Day. But that's James."

"How many people are Deaf in your family?" Charlie asked.

"Millie and I are the only hearing," Oliver said. "Everyone else—Grandpa Sol, Mom, Dad, James, Frog—are Deaf. Well, Dad's hard of hearing, but he's still Deaf."

Mrs. Castle came into the room. She pulled Oliver's comforter to his chin and leaned down to give him a hug, making a humming sound in her throat. His mom quietly kissed him on the cheek. Then Mrs. Castle stood on her tiptoes. She straightened Charlie's comforter, patted his shoulder, and made a sign with her middle fingers folded, and her thumb, forefinger, and pinky extended. She turned off the light and closed the door halfway.

Oliver handed Charlie a small flashlight. "Here you

go—in case you want to read." Charlie turned it on. "Oliver, what does this mean?" Charlie made the sign Mrs. Castle had made.

"I love you," Oliver said. "But in this instance it really means, 'I'm here if you need me.'"

Charlie thought about that. It seemed to him to be the same thing.

The rain pitter-pattered softly outside Oliver's open window. The curtains fluttered in the breeze. Charlie started reading *Dorrie McCann and the Mystery of the Secret Treasure*. He paused before every page turn to practice the "*I-love-you-I'm-here-if-you-need-me*" sign until he was too sleepy to read any longer.

• • •

Charlie woke.

The rain had stopped. It was quiet except for the wind and—Charlie listened carefully—something else was outside.

"Oliver?" Charlie whispered.

Charlie went to the window. The heavy clouds hid the moon. He could just see the outline of the barn below and the stone wall behind it.

Bear nudged open Oliver's door. He padded over to Charlie, a low growl in his throat.

"You hear something, too, Bear?" Charlie whispered.

Bear put his paws on the windowsill, and growled louder.

Oliver woke up. "Bear, quiet!"

"He hears something," Charlie said.

"He always hears things," Oliver said. "Bear, go back to Millie's room."

Charlie and Bear looked at each other, listening.

*CREEEEEAAAAAKKKKK.*

The graveyard door.

Bear barked.

"Shhh!" Oliver rolled over.

Frog would be outraged if Charlie didn't let her know someone might be in the graveyard. Without thinking through how Frog would react, Charlie grabbed the flashlight, tiptoed to her room, and woke her up.

Of course Frog wanted to investigate.

*What if it's Dex and Ray?* Frog wrote. *It's our chance to find them!*

*Exactly. What if it's Dex and Ray? It's dangerous!*

*What if it's Aggie?* Frog wrote.

Charlie hesitated.

Frog pointed to Bear, who was watching Frog closely. *We'll take Bear with us.*

Frog slipped on a golf ball–size emerald ring. She made a fist and punched it forward.

*"Bring your key,"* Frog signed.

It was already in Charlie's hand.

. . .

"Where are you going?" Oliver asked.

"The graveyard," Charlie said as he put on his sneakers.

Oliver sat up. "Great. Now I have to come, too."

"Why?"

"Oh, sure," Oliver said. "A boy who easily does twenty push-ups stays inside, while outside young children face deadly danger?"

"Deadly danger?" Charlie said. "What deadly danger?"

But Oliver just sighed and shook his head.

Outside, Frog held Bear by a tight leash. Charlie's ears pricked at every sound. The squishing noises their shoes made in the muddy ground. The trees rattling in the breeze. Bear's growl.

The sounds, of course, did not distract Frog. Her laser-beam eyes swept the darkness, searching for anything out of the ordinary.

Frog pointed. The graveyard door was open.

"Forget what I said before," Oliver told Charlie, "because now I'm scared." Oliver tucked his flashlight under his armpit. Oliver made fists, and then opened his hands wide, palms facing inward. "*Scared*." Charlie did the same.

Oliver tapped Frog on the shoulder. The two boys signed to her. *"We're scared."*

Frog ignored them both and plowed ahead toward the graveyard.

Charlie's mind raced. What if Dex and Ray were in there? What if flashlights, a key, a golf ball–size ring, and a bear-dog weren't enough to protect them? What if the graveyard really was haunted?

Frog did not appear concerned with what-ifs. She signed for everyone to turn off the flashlights.

The three of them stood outside the graveyard door. It took a minute to adjust to the darkness. The only thing Charlie could hear now was his heart pounding. He gripped his key harder in his sweaty fist.

Frog wrapped Bear's leash one more time around her hand. She made an emerald-ringed fist with her other hand and slipped through the door. Oliver and Charlie followed.

They stayed glued to Frog. She turned on her flashlight but kept the light pointed downward. Bear's ears, eyes, and nose were on high alert.

"*Shhh*," Frog warned. Slowly the group moved forward through the graveyard. When Frog put up a hand, they all froze, including Bear. When she lowered it, they all continued walking.

Frog's light landed on Bernadette Mills's grave.

I TOLD YOU, TOO!

BUT YOU WOULD NOT LISTEN!

Charlie had trouble breathing. He thought about all the dead bodies lying beneath them this very moment. What if dead people don't like you walking on their graves while they're trying to sleep? Do dead people sleep? Or do they get up and do their haunting in the middle of the—

"HOO-HOO!"

"AHHH!" Charlie knocked the flashlight out of Frog's hands.

He heard the sound of running feet. Bear leaped forward, pulling the leash out of Frog's hand, and charged into the darkness.

"Go, go!" a voice shouted.

Frog grabbed her flashlight. She raced after Bear on the path around the headstones, Charlie and Oliver right behind her. At the very back of the graveyard stood Bear on his hind legs, pawing at the wall. Charlie heard car doors slam shut. Frog dropped her flashlight, found toeholds in the wall, and quickly began to climb. An engine started. Just as Frog made it to the top of the wall, Charlie heard the car zoom away. Frog climbed back down.

*"I couldn't see who it was,"* she signed as Oliver interpreted. Frog looked at Charlie, hands on her hips. *"Why did you do that? You scared them away!"*

Oliver signed to her. Frog said, *"An owl? You heard an owl?"*

Charlie had thought it was a ghost. *"I'm sorry,"* he signed.

But Frog didn't see Charlie's sign. She had spotted something on the ground by the wall.

A gum wrapper.

A sugar-free cinnamon gum wrapper.

# 25. Remember

Charlie woke up to banging and thumping noises.

"Uh-oh," Oliver yawned. "Mom's in a mood." He pulled the comforter over his head.

Charlie had just gotten dressed when Frog burst into the bedroom.

"You're supposed to knock!" Charlie gestured. If Frog had come in a few seconds earlier—

"*Sorry!*" Frog signed. She showed Charlie her notepad.

*Remember! Lots of people chew sugar-free cinnamon gum! Lots of people litter!*

It was Frog's reminder of what they had talked about

last night. Frog did not want Charlie to say anything to her parents about Dex and Ray possibly being in the graveyard.

Charlie disagreed. *We know Dex and Ray chew sugar-free cinnamon gum! We know Ray litters!*

*But we don't know for CERTAIN,* Frog pointed out.

More thumping and banging noises.

Frog prodded Oliver, who uncovered an eye and watched her sign. He nodded and sat up. "I hate to say these words, Charlie, but Frog might be right." Oliver rubbed his eyes. "This isn't the best time to say anything to Mom. I mean, just listen to those sounds. I told you— Mom gets intense this time of year." Oliver signed what he had just said to Frog.

*"That,"* Frog signed, which clearly meant, "That's my point!"

The three of them went into the kitchen, where they found Mr. Castle drinking coffee and reading the newspaper. Millie was making peanut-butter-and-jelly sandwiches. Frog brought a box of cereal and milk to the table while Oliver got bowls and spoons.

Mr. Castle lowered his newspaper. "Ah. Frog, Oliver, and Charlie. Good morning," he said and signed. "I was just warning—er, telling Millie that we all need to be extra care—rather, helpful with Mom today because—"

Mrs. Castle stormed into the kitchen.

Charlie hadn't realized you could yell in sign language. But yelling Mrs. Castle was—with large, piercing signs that pinned them to their chairs.

Mr. Castle stood up as if wanting to hug her. Even Charlie could see this wasn't a good idea. Mrs. Castle shot a warning look at Mr. Castle. He sat back down. She continued her yelling.

"Mommy is saying," Millie interpreted for Charlie, "that no one is doing anything else today except helping her get ready for the Founders' Day Dinner."

But what about their investigation? Charlie could see Frog was thinking the same thing because she began arguing with her mother. Mrs. Castle raised one hand—fingers spread wide—and turned it away from her with a sharp twist. Frog crossed her arms and slumped in her chair. Mrs. Castle turned to Charlie and signed.

"Mommy says she isn't yelling at you, Charlie," Millie said. "She's sorry you had to see her get so mad. But there's a lot of work to do, and she is tired of having to do everything herself!"

Mrs. Castle stormed out of the room.

Everyone let out a sigh.

"*Your mother is very worried about Grandpa,*" Mr. Castle signed and then spoke. "*He should have been home last night. We all need to pitch in today. And Millie, are you really going to eat all those sandwiches?*" Mr. Castle returned to his newspaper.

KANE

Millie put her sandwiches in a brown bag as Frog wrote: *See? We can't say anything right now!*

*I hope your grandpa is okay,* Charlie told her.

*Grandpa is fine! He's just late, that's all. But Mom's not going to let me out of her sight today.* Frog brightened. *If I help enough today, maybe tomorrow we can do more investigating.*

*Okay,* Charlie wrote. *Today I have something to do anyway. Something to help me stay in Castle-on-the-Hudson.*

*Remember,* Frog told him. *You're the one with the power.*

Frog showed Charlie the sign for "*remember.*" She signed the letter *A* with both hands, palms down, her thumbs sticking out. Keeping her left hand in front of her body, she touched her right thumb to her forehead and brought it down to touch her left thumb. Charlie copied Frog. "*Remember.*"

Frog crossed her fingers on both of her hands. Charlie did the same.

• • •

"You're going to do what?" Yvette asked.

"Bake cookies," Charlie said. "With Grandma and Grandpa."

"Bake cookies?" Yvette peered into the living room. Charlie's grandparents were sunk in their E-Z chair recliners, staring at a news program. "With them?"

"Yes," Charlie said. "With them."

Yvette picked up her book. "I'll be upstairs dusting."

Charlie read the list of ingredients on the bag of chocolate chips: flour, sugar, eggs, butter, vanilla, baking soda, and salt. He found them all and lined them up on the center island counter. Then he went into the living room and stepped in front of the television.

"Charlie, I can't see the commercial," Grandma Tickler said. "And I love this one—the dog sings." Grandma flipped through the television guide. "Irving, what's on next? That baking show we like?"

"I thought we could do something even better," Charlie said.

"What's better than a baking show?" Grandma asked. "A murder-mystery show?"

"No," Charlie said. "Instead of watching a baking show, *we do* the baking."

"Do?" Grandma said.

"Yes," Charlie said. "And I have the perfect thing for us to make—chocolate chip cookies!"

"Charlie wants to bake us cookies, Irving!" Grandma shouted to Grandpa.

"Not me," Charlie said. "We. We bake cookies *together*."

Charlie turned the television off. He planted his feet wide and folded his arms.

Grandma Tickler got the message first.

"Charlie wants *us* to bake cookies, Irving!" Grandma said. "And he's not going to turn the television back on until we do!"

. . .

After much discussion—Grandma Tickler wanted to move the E-Z chair recliners to the kitchen and sit while baking—Charlie's grandparents were finally standing next to the line of cookie ingredients.

The first step of the recipe said to "cream butter and sugar together."

"What does that mean?" Charlie asked.

"It means to mash together. Isn't that right, Irving?"

"Ayuh." Grandpa Tickler had watched as many baking shows as Grandma Tickler had.

Grandpa Tickler grabbed a fork. He began stabbing at the hard lump of butter.

"Irving, you're not doing it right!" Grandma Tickler grabbed the fork from Grandpa Tickler. Grandpa Tickler grabbed it back. Grandma Tickler was trying to wrestle the fork out of Grandpa Tickler's hand when Charlie had a brilliant idea.

"Grandma! Grandpa! Let's pretend we're on our own baking show!"

Charlie's grandparents froze mid–tug-of-war.

"We can pretend the cookie jar is the camera,"

Charlie said, pointing to the ceramic container next to the oven.

Charlie held up his hand and counted down with his fingers. "Our baking show starts in three, two, one. Action! Hello, everyone. I'm Charlie Tickler. I'm here with my grandparents, Irma and Irving Tickler, on the very first episode of *Baking with the Grandkids.*"

Grandma and Grandpa Tickler stared at the cookie jar. They did not blink.

Charlie continued. "They're wonderful grandparents because they're taking time to bake with me, their *only* grandson, Charlie. And we are going to bake the most delicious cookies you have ever tasted in your life!"

Grandma and Grandpa both nodded at the cookie jar.

"Right now my grandpa is creaming the butter."

Grandpa Tickler resumed his stabbing.

"Charlie said cream the butter, not kill it!" Grandma Tickler said.

Grandpa Tickler pointed the fork at Grandma. "Ayuh!"

"Irving!" Grandma Tickler said. "How about I stick a fork in *you*?!"

"Remember we're on TV," Charlie whispered. Grandpa stabbed the fork back into the butter.

Charlie read the next step. "Sift flour, salt, and baking soda together. Do you know what 'sift' means, Grandma?" Charlie asked.

"Of course I know!" Grandma said. "Hand me the sifter!"

"What's a sifter?" Charlie asked.

"A sifter is for sifting!"

"Do you have a sifter?" Charlie asked.

"I don't think so," Grandma said. "Better skip that part."

Charlie handed her a measuring cup. "Two and a quarter cups of flour, Grandma."

Grandma began scooping flour. She spilled quite a bit since she was looking at the cookie jar camera and not at the mixing bowl.

The baking-show people always talked as they cooked, so while Charlie's grandparents stabbed and scooped, Charlie narrated. "Cooking with your grand-kids is important. Right, Grandma and Grandpa?"

"Ayuh," Grandpa said.

"Depends," Grandma said.

"On what?" Charlie asked.

"If the cookies taste good!"

They added the rest of the ingredients, mixing in the chocolate chips last. Charlie helped his grandparents form the lumpy dough into balls. He placed them on a baking sheet. Then Grandma and Grandpa hustled back to their E-Z chair recliners. Charlie joined them in the living room while the cookies baked.

The house started to smell wonderful. Charlie took some big loud sniffs to encourage Grandma and Grandpa Tickler to do the same.

"Tissues are in the bathroom," Grandma Tickler told Charlie.

Charlie sighed and leaned back on the couch. It was hard being on a baking show when you didn't know how to bake and your fellow bakers didn't *want* to bake. But maybe it would work. Maybe it would make his grandparents care about him.

Charlie thought about what Frog had said in the graveyard. *They have to care! That's what it means to be a family—you have to care!*

Charlie wondered why some kids had family who cared, like Frog. And why some kids had family who just didn't, like Charlie.

Maybe it was his fault. Maybe there was something wrong with him.

Someone else began sniffing. Someone else finally smelled the cookies, too!

It was Yvette, coming down the stairs. "Something's burning."

Charlie ran into the kitchen. He put on an oven mitt and pulled out a pan of burnt cookies. Yvette opened the back door to let out the smoke. After the smoke cleared Yvette served Charlie's grandparents the lemon squares she had made the day before. Grandma and Grandpa Tickler enjoyed them immensely while watching a baking show from their E-Z chair recliners.

# 26. Sweetheart

Miss Tweedy was at the circulation desk, sipping peach iced tea. Charlie handed her *Baking with the Grandkids: 101 Easy Recipes to Fill Their Stomachs and Your Heart.*

It was time to be blunt.

"Your grandparents may have loved to read and bake," Charlie said, "but my grandparents love to watch television. They can do that without me. I need to find something they can do *with* me."

Miss Tweedy took the white card from the back of the baking book, thwacked it with the ink stamp, and slipped the card back in its holder.

"Well," Miss Tweedy said, "there was something my

grandfather loved to do, but with my younger sister, Enid. It was much too violent for me."

She pulled a book off a cart next to the circulation desk. *Fishing: The Basics.*

"Fishing?" Charlie said. "Fishing is violent?"

"Oh yes. The impaling of the worm. The glint of the steel hook. The thrashing of the fish. Horrendous." Miss Tweedy shuddered. "Pancake Pond is stocked with fish for the violent taking. Enid loves to fish and knit. She can do both at the same time, you know."

There is a lot of sitting and watching with fishing—skills Charlie's grandparents had already mastered. Fishing was perfect.

Charlie needed one more book. Miss Tweedy had found the fishing book for him. This time she looked pointedly at the card catalog. Charlie pulled out the drawer labeled *Aa–As*. He found the title he wanted. He showed the Dewey decimal number (419.7) to Miss Tweedy.

"In the Dewey decimal system," Miss Tweedy said, "four hundred and nineteen means sign languages. Add a decimal point and a seven, and you have the Dewey decimal number for American Sign Language. You'll find the book *ASL? You Can!* on the shelves by the grandfather clock."

It was a fat, heavy book. Mrs. Castle had said there was more to ASL than just signs. Charlie hoped this book would show him what Mrs. Castle had meant. He handed Miss Tweedy his library card and checked out both books.

Charlie sat down in the squishy armchair in the front of the library. He pulled out the letter from Frog that Mr. Simple had delivered this morning.

> *Dear Charlie,*
>
> *All I have done since you left is CLEAN! But Oliver did distract Mom long enough for me to sneak away and investigate the grave-yard. Stop worrying! I brought Bear with me!*
>
> *I regret to report I did not find any dead bodies except for the ones already buried. And I didn't find any blood or any other clues that explain why Dex and Ray came here or what Aggie could have meant when she signed "dead."*
>
> *BUT Dad said I could go to the village today when Mom is out doing errands!!!*
>
> *Can you meet at the library at 12:30 p.m. to figure out the next step in our investigation?*
>
> *Sincerely,*
> *Frog*

Charlie had an idea. In his yearbook Grandpa Sol had said he loved to fish. And because Grandpa

Sol sounded like the kind of grandparent who did things with his grandchildren, Charlie bet Frog knew how to fish, too.

Charlie tore out a few sheets of paper from his notebook. Using the ASL book, he drew a picture of himself signing "*fish*." Charlie only had a blue pen, so he couldn't show the color of his hair or eyes. But he could draw his freckles and his cowlick standing straight up like it always did—no matter how much he combed his hair. He studied his picture. Charlie added a drawing of a fish in case it wasn't clear what his hands were doing. Underneath he wrote:

> *Frog,*
> *Can you come fishing with my grand-parents and me? If yes, meet me at my grandparents' house at 12:30 p.m. instead of meeting at the library.*
> *Thanks, Charlie*

Charlie was torn between finding Aggie and making sure he didn't find himself being shipped off to boarding school.

> *PS: We'll continue our investigation right after fishing.*
> *PPS: Bring fishing poles if you have them.*

Charlie walked to the gondola station, where Mr. Simple was reading a magazine while impatient riders waited. He handed him the folded notepaper. Mr. Simple nodded his approval when Charlie gave him three dollars for Frog's tip. Charlie did, after all, have lots of change left from his hundred-dollar bill.

• • •

"You're going to do what?" Yvette asked.

"Go fishing," Charlie said. "With Grandma and Grandpa."

"Fishing?" Yvette eyed the empty E-Z chair recliners. Charlie's grandparents were at a doctor's appointment. "With them?"

"Yes," Charlie said, "with them."

Yvette felt Charlie's forehead. "Do you have a fever?"

Frog knocked on the door just as Yvette was getting a thermometer. A glittering goldfish was pinned to her T-shirt. She handed Charlie two fishing poles and pulled out her notepad and pen.

*Why are we fishing?* Frog wrote. *We need to be investigating!*

*It's part of my plan*, Charlie told her, *to get my grandparents to want me to stay.*

Frog nodded and crossed her fingers once again. Charlie did, too, even though it hadn't worked last time.

*The hardest part will be getting my grandparents away from the TV,* Charlie explained. *They watch TV all day—except when they have a doctor's appointment.*

NO WAY, Frog spelled.

WAY, Charlie replied.

Frog thought a moment. *My grandpa likes to hike.*

Charlie imagined his grandparents on a mountain trail—sitting in their E-Z chair recliners.

*Not happening,* Charlie wrote.

• • •

Yvette solved the problem of getting Charlie's grandparents out of their E-Z chair recliners—she didn't let them sit in the E-Z chair recliners in the first place. Instead, when Herman returned the Ticklers from their doctor's appointment, Yvette, Charlie, and Frog blocked the taxi doors.

"What are you doing?" Grandma Tickler protested. "It's lunchtime! We need to get out and eat!"

Yvette held up a lunch basket. "I've got your lunch right here. You're going fishing—with Charlie and Frog."

"Yvette said we have to fish for our lunch," Grandma Tickler shouted to Grandpa Tickler. "With Charlie and Toad!"

"Frog, Grandma. Her name is Frog!"

• • •

They drove to Pancake Pond, on the outskirts of the village. As Herman's taxi rattled away Charlie set up lawn chairs and Frog stuck worms on hooks. Frog tapped Grandpa Tickler on the shoulder to make sure he was looking at her. Then, with gestures, she showed Grandpa Tickler how to cast the fishing line.

Grandpa placed the fishing pole between his knees. Slowly he raised both hands, and with both hands signed the letter *A*. He brought his knuckles together over his heart, and wiggled his thumbs.

Frog and Charlie stared at Grandpa Tickler in astonishment.

Frog fingerspelled to Charlie what that sign meant. SWEETHEART.

"Sweetheart?" Charlie said. He made the sign himself.

"Sweetheart," Grandma Tickler confirmed as she reeled in pondweed. "Irving's telling you he had a sweetheart who went to that Castle School—that's the one sign he remembers!"

Charlie wrote down what Grandma Tickler said. Frog read it and laughed.

*"Who was your sweetheart?"* Frog signed to Grandpa Tickler. Charlie voiced Frog's question to make sure Grandpa understood.

"It was Mabel." Grandma Tickler answered for Grandpa Tickler. "Mabel with the big head. That girl had the biggest head I've ever seen. Now why haven't we caught any fish yet?"

"You have to be patient, Grandma," Charlie said after he had written down for Frog what Grandma had said. "We just started. Here, have a sandwich." Charlie reached into the picnic basket Yvette had packed. He handed Grandma Tickler a sandwich wrapped in wax paper.

"Do you know why we are fishing, Grandma?" Charlie asked.

"To catch fish!"

"Not just to catch fish," Charlie said. "It's to do something together. That's what grandparents and grandchildren are supposed to do—things together."

Grandma Tickler mulled this over as she took a large bite of her egg salad sandwich.

"Ayuh," Grandpa said.

"That's true, Irving," Grandma Tickler agreed. "Mabel *was* a wonderful girl even if she did have a big head. It's wonderful you are learning sign language, Charlie. Sweethearts should understand each other!"

"Grandma! Frog is not my sweetheart!"

"*What?*" Frog signed.

Charlie did not want to write down for Frog what Grandma Tickler had just said. He almost wrote "never mind" before he realized how rude that would be. Frog had a right to know.

So Charlie wrote it down.

*WHAT?* Frog stared at Charlie. *WE ARE NOT SWEETHEARTS!!!*

*I TOLD HER THAT!!!*

*GOOD!!!*

"Are there any potato chips, Charlie?" Grandma Tickler asked. "Egg salad sandwiches need potato chips."

Charlie opened the bag of chips Yvette had packed.

"I especially remember Mabel's friend," Grandma Tickler said. She opened her egg salad sandwich and placed several potato chips inside. "She was so tiny. And she was always knitting Irving scarves and such!"

Knitting?

Charlie wrote this down. Frog began hopping up and down on one foot. She urged Charlie to keep up his questioning.

"Grandma, do you remember her name?" Charlie asked.

"No," Grandma Tickler said. "I do not remember her name. But I remember that big mole on her face. That's how I recognized her this morning." Grandma Tickler took a crunchy bite of egg-salad-potato-chip sandwich.

"This morning?" Charlie said. "You saw her *this* morning?"

Charlie scribbled this down. Frog started jumping up and down with both feet.

"Grandma, was her name Aggie?" Charlie spelled her name as he spoke it.

"That was her name!" Grandma Tickler nodded. "Aggie Penderwick."

NO WAY! Frog spelled.

"Did she look okay?" Charlie asked.

"She looked perfectly fine. Just worried. Isn't that right, Irving?"

"Ayuh," Grandpa Tickler said.

"Tell us what happened, Grandma," Charlie said.

"Well, Irving and I were headed to our doctor's appointment to get our hearing checked—both of us, both ears. When Herman's taxi stopped at a red light, I saw Aggie on the sidewalk. I said, 'Isn't that the woman who was always knitting you scarves and such?' Didn't I say that, Irving?"

"Ayuh," Grandpa Tickler said.

"So I waved to Aggie—just to be polite, you know. She came over to our taxi. That's when we saw she was worried about something. But we couldn't understand what she was trying to tell us because Irving only remembers the sign for 'sweetheart.' Isn't that right, Irving?"

"Ayuh," Grandpa Tickler agreed.

"So Aggie quickly wrote on a notepad *looking for a*

*book* and *waiting for Sol Castle*," Grandma Tickler said. "But we had no idea what that meant!"

Charlie scribbled down what Grandma was saying as fast as he could for Frog.

"Irving gestured for Aggie to get into the taxi, but then the light turned green," Grandma Tickler continued. "Herman started driving away, because that's what Herman does when lights turn green. But Aggie didn't want to get in. She just hurried off. She acted very mysterious. Aggie always did love mysteries, didn't she, Irving?"

"Ayuh," Grandpa Tickler said.

Charlie and Frog asked Grandma and Grandpa Tickler to tell them more about meeting Aggie. Neither one could recall anything else.

*At least we know Aggie is okay,* Charlie wrote.

*For now,* Frog replied. *And we know Aggie is looking for a book. And we know why Aggie was at the castle—she was looking for Grandpa Sol. But why? How can Grandpa help her?*

*Maybe Grandpa Sol knows about the book Aggie is looking for,* Charlie suggested.

Charlie and Frog debated where to investigate next. Should they go back to the castle? The graveyard? The village? And what book was Aggie looking for? How did a book connect to the secret Aggie had told?

Miss Tweedy had promised violence and bonding

over fishing. Nothing of the sort happened. In fact nothing much happened at all—although Grandma and Grandpa Tickler did manage to nap while holding their fishing poles.

When Herman arrived to bring them home, he handed a letter to Frog that Mr. Simple had passed on to him.

> *Frog,*
>
> *Your mother is back from her errands and agitated that you are not here. Please come home as soon as you receive this note. There is much cleaning still to be done.*
> *XO, Dad*

Herman drove by the gondola station before taking Charlie and his grandparents home. He didn't come to a complete stop, but he did drive slowly enough for Frog to jump out with the fishing poles.

# 27. Same-Same

"Such an adventure!" Grandma Tickler said as Yvette served their dinner on TV trays. "Driving to the pond, sitting by the pond, throwing worms into the pond. An adventure, I tell you!"

Grandma Tickler settled back in her E-Z chair recliner with a satisfied sigh.

"Ayuh," Grandpa said.

"It doesn't matter that we didn't catch any fish, Irving," Grandma Tickler said. "The point of fishing is to do something together. Isn't that right, Charlie?"

"That's right, Grandma!" Charlie said as he carried in silverware and napkins from the kitchen.

"I never thought I'd see the day when Irma and Irving Tickler went fishing," Yvette said. She placed a glass of milk on each of their trays. "This is the most fun I've had since I started working here."

"Exactly!" Charlie said. "Having a grandson around is fun!"

"But not too much fun, Charlie." Grandma Tickler speared something white and drippy from her plate. "Too much fun, like too much of anything, is never a good thing. We need to recover from all the excitement of today. Next year, though, we'll be ready to fish again, won't we, Irving?"

"But, Grandma—"

"Hush, Charlie! Our show is about to start."

. . .

Charlie and Yvette ate their dinner in the kitchen. The white, drippy noodle casserole Yvette had made looked disgusting, but tasted delicious. As Charlie ate he thought about his grandparents and their self-defense moves.

How they had jumped out of their chairs.

How they had circled each other.

How they had seemed so different.

"Yvette, do you think people can change?" Charlie asked.

"Nope," Yvette said. She picked up her cup of coffee and took a sip.

"Okay, not change then," Charlie said. "But what if someone has something hidden deep down inside, like Frog. On the outside Frog is an average girl, but on the inside she's an amazing detective who can solve puzzling cases. Or will solve them," Charlie added, crossing his fingers as he thought about Aggie.

"Or Grandma and Grandpa Tickler?" Charlie hurried on before Yvette could say anything. "On the outside they look like boring grandparents, but on the inside they're really ... ninja warriors or something! And they just need help bringing that part of them out!"

"Charlie." Yvette put down her coffee cup. "I'm going to say this because it has to be said. Outside and inside, there isn't anything your grandparents like doing except watching television, eating, and visiting doctors."

"Frog says we have power," Charlie said. "Power to ... to do stuff!"

"Charlie, do you know this sign?"

Yvette signed the letter *Y* with both hands. She made circles with her hands, bringing them away from and then toward each other, pausing a slight bit every time she completed a circle.

"A lady I used to work for would sign this about her husband," Yvette said. "She called this sign 'same-same.'

In English we say, 'Same old, same old.' She meant her husband would never change. That's how it is with your grandparents." Yvette signed it again. "*Same-same.*"

Charlie copied the sign, though he refused to believe it. He still had time to convince his grandparents to want him to stay. Just like he and Frog still had time to find Aggie.

Charlie stood up to clear his plate. "I have to finish reading a book Frog gave me," he said. He had promised Frog, after all.

Yvette touched his arm. "Bring the book down here," she said, "and read aloud while I do the dishes."

. . .

Charlie explained to Yvette what had happened so far in *Dorrie McCann and the Mystery of the Secret Treasure.* Then he began to read:

"*The chief of police looked at his watch. Time was running out. Dorrie McCann needed to decipher the final secret message before it was too late.*

"*Suddenly Dorrie stood up. She reached inside her leather bag and pulled out a long red scarf. She wrapped the scarf around her neck and closed her eyes.*

"'*What is she doing?' the chief demanded. 'I need Dorrie to solve this last cipher right now! Plus, it's hot in here. Why does she need a scarf?'*

*"'The scarf isn't to keep her warm,' Jack explained. 'The scarf is to remind Dorrie to look inside herself and find her own power.'"*

Charlie stopped reading.

"What's wrong?" Yvette asked.

"Nothing," Charlie said.

"Then keep reading!"

But there was something important in what Charlie had just read. What was it? Something he had seen before? Charlie shook his head and kept reading.

. . .

In the middle of the night, Charlie woke up. He knew what the something important was.

Aggie's knitting bag rested on top of his dresser. Charlie got out of bed and went to the bag. Whatever Aggie had been knitting was wrapped around the ball of yarn. Charlie pulled out Aggie's knitting needles, and let her work unfurl.

A long red scarf hung to the floor.

## 28. Wait!

Frog stared at Aggie's scarf and then at Charlie in disbelief. Finally she picked up her pen. *How could you not have noticed Aggie was knitting a red scarf?!*

Charlie was sorry he hadn't noticed what Aggie had been knitting—but seriously? How could Charlie have known that would be important?

Frog reached again into the knitting bag, and pulled out Aggie's note—the note Aggie had written to Miss Tweedy and Charlie, telling them she had told a secret.

*And you never showed me this note, either!* Frog wrote. But Charlie had already told Frog everything that was in the note. But he knew better than to point this out to Frog.

Frog placed the scarf and note gently back into Aggie's knitting bag.

*Every Dorrie McCann fan knows about the red scarf. It's her statement piece! D. J. McKinnon had a scarf just like it from her mother. Her mother told her to wear it and believe in her own power. D.J. wrote all her books wearing her red scarf.*

Charlie thought about the yearbook. *D.J. and Aggie were in the same class*, he wrote. *Maybe Aggie knows who burned D. J. McKinnon's manuscript. She's afraid something like that will happen again with the secret she told. Aggie said theft or destruction could happen. Burning something means destroying it.*

Frog paced her bedroom, twisting her long pearl necklace around her hand before she grabbed her pen again.

*Aggie is knitting a red scarf. The red scarf could be a clue about D. J. McKinnon. Aggie also signed "dead." The sign "dead" could be a clue about the graveyard. So that means Aggie's secret could be . . .*

Frog chewed on the end of her pen.

*. . . a buried treasure hidden inside D. J. McKinnon's grave! We need a shovel!*

*Whoa! Let's just LOOK first!* Charlie wrote.

Frog ignored this. *We have to investigate the graveyard.*

*But I'm supposed to be helping set up for the Founders' Day Dinner. I'm lucky Mom even let me come talk to you!*

Frog paced the room once, and then wrote: *We're close to cracking this case. I feel it.*

Frog touched her fingertips just under her rib cage.

Charlie got it.

*"Intuition."*

Detective intuition.

• • •

Frog peered around the corner and looked down into the great hall. Mrs. Castle was directing Nate Marsh where to set up round tables for the Founders' Day Dinner. When her mother's back was turned, Frog waved to get Oliver's attention.

Frog signed. Oliver nodded.

Oliver went over to his mother and, making sure she faced away from the stairs, engaged her in conversation. Charlie and Frog raced down the steps, Charlie with his key between his knuckles.

Frog sprinted toward the graveyard. Charlie followed at her heels. Suddenly Frog veered off when they came to the barn. She ran inside and came out holding a shovel.

*"No!"* Charlie signed.

*"Yes!"* Frog insisted.

*"No!"*

*"Yes!"*

Frog began running again. She didn't hesitate when they reached the graveyard door set inside the stone wall. She pulled it open in a single swing. A piercing squeal screeched from the rusted hinges.

In the bright light of the sunny day, the graveyard didn't seem nearly as scary as it had in the night. A robin swooped by and settled in a tree. Pale yellow flowers decorated a headstone.

A squirrel, perched on Edward Hyde [NO ONE EVER LISTENS (SIGH), UNTIL IT IS TOO LATE], froze as they passed by.

Charlie and Frog searched for any sign of Aggie or Dex and Ray. Nothing seemed out of the ordinary.

*"Same-same,"* Frog signed, and then wrote: *Everything is the same as it was before, when I investigated the graveyard with Bear.*

As they followed the winding path to the back of the graveyard, Frog hoisted the shovel with a determined look. Charlie scrawled a hasty note as they walked.

*Frog, we cannot dig up D. J. McKinnon's grave!*

*"Can,"* Frog signed.

*"Can't!"* Charlie signed back.

Someone had left a red flower next to D. J. McKinnon's headstone. Charlie remembered Mr. Simple had said that former students liked to come early, before the annual Founders' Day Dinner, to visit their favorite author's grave. One of them must have left the flower there.

Frog did not seem to notice the red flower. Instead she walked around the headstone, testing the ground with the end of her shovel, searching for the best place to start digging.

Charlie held his notebook up to Frog's face. *WAIT! HOW DO YOU SIGN "WAIT"?*

Frog sighed. She leaned the shovel against her chest. She held up her hands, palms facing inward, one hand slightly closer to her body, and wiggled her fingers. "*Wait.*"

"*Why?*" Frog signed.

Good question.

Because they would get in so much trouble? Because digging up a body was against the law? Because Charlie did not want to see the inside of a grave? Charlie knew none of these reasons would be good enough for—

Charlie bent down. The flower on D. J. McKinnon's grave wasn't a real flower. It was a red knitted flower. The flower Aggie had been wearing the day Charlie had met her.

Charlie picked up the flower pin and handed it to Frog. *This is Aggie's!*

Frog rubbed the knitted flower with her fingertips.

*You never told me Aggie was wearing a statement piece!*

How could Charlie have known a statement piece would be important? He didn't even know what a statement piece *was* before he met Frog. But Frog wasn't mad—the flower pin seemed to confirm something for her.

*This proves Aggie is connected to D. J. McKinnon!* Frog wrote. *And D. J. McKinnon is in the graveyard—that means this IS a murder mystery!*

*Are you saying D.J. was murdered?!*

*No! Yes! I don't know! But we have to DO something. Good people act!*

Frog raised her shovel high, ready to dig. Charlie grabbed the shovel handle with one hand and with his other hand signed, *"Wait!"*

*Dorrie McCann and the Mystery of the Secret Treasure* whirled through Charlie's mind. He let go of the shovel and signed, *"Wait!"* one more time. He quickly wrote: *What if there's something on D.J.'s headstone? Like a secret code?*

CIPHER, Frog spelled.

*"That,"* Charlie signed.

Frog lowered her shovel and nodded.

The letters on D. J. McKinnon's headstone inscription were all engraved differently: Some were swirly, some were plain. Some thick, some thin. Some large, some small.

*Why are the letters that way?* Charlie asked.

*It's different kinds of fonts. She was a printer, remember? It was a way to honor her work. Look for patterns and write them down.*

Charlie wrote down the whole inscription. Then he studied the headstone. The year she was born and the year she died were written in the regular way. But the next line read:

DIED ON THE 4TH DAY OF THE 1ST MONTH, AT THE 9.TH HOUR AND 7TH MINUTE.

*That's a weird way to write when she died,* Charlie wrote.

*It isn't weird! It's unique!* But Frog looked at the numbers closely. *The numbers of the day, month, hour, and minute are all in the same font. But not the years.*

Charlie wrote down the numbers of the day, month, hour, and minute together. **4197**. Frog pointed to the engraved line below the date D. J. McKinnon died.

DEAREST DAUGHTER AND LOYAL FRIEND

Frog tapped the *r* in "dearest," the *e* in "daughter," and the *f* in "friend." *REF.* Those three letters were in the same font as the numbers of the day, month, hour, and minute. Charlie wrote down *REF* next to the day, month, hour, and minute numbers. **4197** REF.

Charlie and Frog continued to study the headstone. Charlie wrote down any letters that were in the same kind of font together. Finally they sat back on their heels and studied Charlie's paper. It seemed just a jumble of letters and numbers.

Frog sighed. *I have no idea! I need Dorrie's scarf!* Frog fell back onto the grass. Charlie joined her. Together they gazed at the blue sky. A soft breeze blew. A robin trilled from a tree above them. Frog sat up and grabbed the pen.

*We need to go back to the beginning. Aggie went to the village library. Dex and Ray went to the village library. We KNOW Aggie is looking for a book. Maybe these letters and numbers will guide us once we're at the library.*

*But*, Charlie protested, *you aren't allowed to go anywhere!*

Frog stood. *We have to!* She pulled Charlie to his feet. *Aggie needs us. Besides, a true detective would never stop an investigation just because she might be grounded for eternity!*

• • •

For once the gondola ride was smooth and easy. Charlie and Frog were the first ones off. When they reached the library, Miss Tweedy was checking out books to a father and son. Charlie and Frog flopped in the squishy chairs in the front of the library, breathing hard. Mr. Dickens eyed them with exasperation.

When Frog had caught her breath she wrote: *Okay. We're here! Where do we start?*

*You're asking me? What about Deaf can?!*

*I said let's go to the graveyard! I said let's come to the library! It's time for hearing can!*

Fair enough. Charlie wiped his forehead and studied the paper. The letters and numbers were still a jumble.

Charlie took a deep breath. *Okay. A library is filled with letters and numbers. Not as many numbers as letters, though. So let's look at the numbers we wrote down first.*

Charlie pointed to the numbers of the day, month, hour, and minute. *These were written in a unique way. Maybe it means something.*

Charlie and Frog studied how D.J.'s death had been recorded.

Died on the *4*th Day of the *1*st Month, at the *9*.th Hour and 7th Minute.

Below Charlie had written out the numbers by themselves, plus *REF* because those three letters were in the same kind of font.

**4197** REF.

*What's this?* Frog pointed to the inscription.

When Charlie had copied down the inscription, he had put a period after the nine because that was what he saw on the headstone: *9.th hour.*

*It's a period*, Charlie wrote.

*But why?* Frog asked. *Why is there a period?*

Charlie looked around the library and then back at the number. *Miss Tweedy explained to me about Dewey decimal numbers.*

*So?* Frog wrote.

*So what if it's not a period?* Charlie replied. *What if it's—*

*A decimal point! Of course!*

Charlie added the decimal point after the nine.

**419.7** REF

Wait. Charlie knew this number. *This is the same Dewey decimal number as my ASL book! Could my ASL book be the one we're looking for?*

Frog bounced up and down in her chair. *Maybe! Or another ASL book! Books about the same subject have the same Dewey decimal number. Let's look!*

Charlie and Frog went to the shelves by the grandfather clock, where Charlie had found his ASL book. They studied the spine of each book. There were no books with the Dewey decimal number 419.7.

They hurried to the circulation desk.

"Miss Tweedy, can you check if someone else besides me borrowed a book with this Dewey decimal number?" Charlie asked.

Miss Tweedy looked at Charlie's paper. "Absolutely not!" She shook her head vehemently and gave the circulation desk a couple of hard pounds with her fist—"absolutely not" in Tweedy Sign Language.

"*Why?*" Frog signed.

"Frog Castle, what kind of a librarian do you think I am?" Miss Tweedy did some TSL finger waves. "I would never allow that!"

"*Why?*" Frog patiently asked again.

"Because," Miss Tweedy said, "even though this book has the Dewey decimal number 419.7, it is also a reference book." Miss Tweedy's finger jabbed at the letters *REF* Charlie had written down next to 419.7. "*REF* means reference! Reference books stay in the library at all times. Reference books may not be checked out!"

Charlie wrote this down for Frog. Then he realized— if the book they were looking for was a reference book, it must still be in the library. Charlie was about to ask where to find the reference section when Frog beat him to it.

"*Where?*" Frog signed.

"Reference books are over there." Miss Tweedy pointed to the section of the library Aggie had been in. "However"—Miss Tweedy shook her head and waved her finger—"you will not find the book."

"*WHY?*" Charlie and Frog both shouted in sign.

"Because," Miss Tweedy said, "it was stolen from the library."

# 29. Stolen

*"Stolen?"*

Frog slid the letter *V* up the outside of her opposite forearm while bending her fingers. Both Charlie and Miss Tweedy copied Frog's sign. *"Stolen."*

*"When?"* Charlie and Frog signed.

Miss Tweedy started to use TSL. Frog stopped her. Tweedy Sign Language, unlike a real language like ASL, wasn't enough for Miss Tweedy to tell her tale. Instead Charlie wrote furiously as Miss Tweedy used the one language she did know fluently.

"Yesterday," Miss Tweedy spoke in English, "two men came into the library. They went to the four hundred section. When they couldn't find the book they were looking for they came to me. They told me the Dewey decimal number. I knew exactly which book they wanted."

Miss Tweedy stopped talking so Charlie could catch up.

*"How did you know?"* Frog signed.

"I knew," Miss Tweedy said, "because I always remember numbers *and* because of Vince Vinelli and Harold Woo."

"Vince Vinelli?" Charlie said as he scribbled. Frog's eyes lit up when she saw his name.

"Oh, yes," Miss Tweedy said. "Vince Vinelli says good people do good things. So I would come to the library and dust books because"—Miss Tweedy looked at the portrait above the fireplace—"Harold hated to dust." She dabbed her eyes with a tissue.

Frog gave Miss Tweedy's arm a patient pat. Charlie and Frog waited for Miss Tweedy to go on because none of this made any sense yet.

"One day," Miss Tweedy continued, "I was dusting the reference section. I was on a chair, cleaning the very top shelf. I noticed one book had been assigned the wrong Dewey decimal number. I didn't even need to open the book to know the number was wrong. The Dewey decimal number was four one nine point seven—an American Sign Language book. Our library has many ASL books, all currently checked out because they are very popular—Charlie has one of them! Harold Woo made this particular ASL book a reference book. What puzzled me, however, was the title of this book had nothing to do with ASL. It had to do with something horrendous!

"'Harold,' I said, 'this Dewey decimal number is wrong.' 'Elspeth,' Harold replied, 'leave it be.' 'But, Harold,' I said, 'the Dewey decimal number is four one nine point seven. It cannot be right.'

"'Elspeth,' Harold said, 'put the book back.' And that was all he would say. He would not tell me why the Dewey decimal number was allowed to be wrong. So that's how I knew that was the book those men wanted. They simply did not seem the sort who would want an ASL book. They seemed the sort who wanted a horrendous book."

Miss Tweedy blew her nose loudly into her tissue.

Charlie's hand was cramping he was writing so fast. Finally he got it all down. Charlie spoke and Frog signed the same question: "*What was the name of the book?*"

"The name of the book was"—Miss Tweedy's voice dropped to a whisper—"*A Dead Author and Her Secret Treasure*." Miss Tweedy shuddered.

"Why is that a horrendous book?" Charlie asked after he had written that down.

"Anything with the word 'dead' is horrendous!" Miss Tweedy said.

This had to be the book Aggie had been looking for

the day Charlie met her! Charlie shook out his left hand and gripped his pen once more.

"So you see," Miss Tweedy said, "I knew about that book even though I hadn't thought about it since Harold left us and I took over his duties. I told the men the name of the book and directed them to the reference section. I couldn't show them myself because at that very moment it was imperative, absolutely imperative, that I visit Mrs. Murphy."

Charlie finished writing that last sentence and decided he had to ask. "Miss Tweedy, why doesn't Mrs. Murphy"—Charlie pointed to her name—"ever visit you?" Charlie pointed to Miss Tweedy.

Frog gave Charlie a stop-talking-right-now look as she signed something down by her leg. "*Bathroom.*" Frog was signing "*bathroom.*"

Bathroom? Visiting Mrs. Murphy was a secret code for "bathroom"?

Oh.

"As I was saying, *Charles*," Miss Tweedy said in a frosty voice, "I had no one to watch the circulation desk for me. You certainly weren't here! When I came back the two men were gone. I went to the reference section, and the book was gone, too! There is no worse crime than stealing a book!"

"Actually," Charlie said, "I can think of a lot worse—"

Miss Tweedy gave him a cold look. Once again Charlie stopped talking.

# 30. Strange

Charlie and Frog sat on the library steps, the same place Charlie had sat with Aggie. They looked at each other in amazement. They couldn't believe it—their detective work had paid off! They had found what Aggie (and Dex and Ray) were looking for.

Well, not really *found* because it wasn't there anymore. But they *knew* what it was.

A kid on a skateboard flew by. He waved to Frog, pointed to Charlie, and signed, *"Who?"* He turned his head backward so he could watch Frog's answer.

Charlie wondered how Frog had answered the question. Did she say, *"This is my friend Charlie"*? Maybe

Frog had simply said what's true: *"This is Charlie, a boy helping me solve a mystery to put on my résumé before he leaves."*

Because Charlie was sure, just in the short time he had known her, that Frog already had a million friends. She definitely didn't need one more.

Frog was writing something. Charlie forced himself to focus on her words.

*Dex and Ray only stole the book yesterday,* Frog pointed out. *So why didn't Aggie find the* Dead *book when she first looked for it?*

*And,* Charlie added, *why would Dex and Ray steal a book? This mystery is very strange.*

Frog's eyes gleamed. *You mean MURDER mystery! The book IS about a dead author!*

*Dead doesn't mean murder!*

*Denial,* Frog wrote. *It's a powerful thing.*

Charlie realized something. *When I saw Aggie signing "dead," I bet she was telling me the name of the book. I wish we knew where she was.*

*We'll find her!* Frog assured him. *Blythe and Bone might have the book. Let's go!*

• • •

Thelonious Bone glared at Frog when they entered the shop. He obviously hadn't forgiven Frog for suggesting that his friend Harold Woo had been poisoned. Matilda Blythe, however, greeted them each with a warm hug.

Once again one of them was left out of the conversation. This time it was Charlie.

Charlie watched Frog sign to Matilda. He knew, of course, what Frog would be asking her. Matilda's eyebrows furrowed. She signed the letter *C*, and with a flick of her wrist, swooped the *C* downward across the middle of her face.

"What's that mean?" Charlie asked as he copied the sign.

"It means 'strange,'" Matilda said. "Strange because two guys asked for that exact same book yesterday."

Frog signed to Matilda, who signed back and then interpreted what she had just said for Charlie. "They didn't buy it because we don't have it. And I couldn't find any information about the book anywhere, so I asked Bone. He also said something strange. He told me some books aren't meant to be read."

Frog signed. Matilda replied, and then said to Charlie, "Bone didn't explain what he meant. But Bone can be a book snob. I'll ask again."

Matilda stamped on the wooden floor twice. Bone looked up with a scowl. Matilda signed to him. Bone's scowl deepened. He held his palm facing inward, fingers spread wide. Then he turned his palm outward with a sharp twist. Charlie remembered Mrs. Castle had made the same sign to Frog. With the same face, too.

Matilda shrugged, signed something to Frog, and then went to ring up a customer. Frog thought for a moment. Her face lit up.

*Dex and Ray,* Frog wrote, *told Matilda the author of the book is D. J. McKinnon. I thought I had every book written by her. I don't have the* Dead Author *book, but I know where we can find it. Hint: It's in the castle!*

Frog waited for Charlie to figure it out. Charlie thought for a moment.

Question: Where did you find books in the castle?

Answer: In the school library.

Except the school library was locked. And they had no way to get in without the key.

Then Charlie remembered—in his study, Grandpa Sol had a copy of every book written by a graduate of Castle School for the Deaf.

. . .

Charlie and Frog arrived just as Mr. Simple was getting ready to close the gondola door. They were both quiet as the gondola swayed over the Hudson River. They were closer and closer to solving the mystery. Charlie couldn't believe they were actually doing it.

Frog led the way to a back entrance of the castle—through hallways and up a narrow staircase to the superintendent's study. Frog cautiously opened the door. Her father was not there. Dust motes hovered in the sunlight streaming through the windows. Frog pointed to the top shelves next to the fireplace. That's where Grandpa kept alumni books. Charlie went to the tall rolling ladder. He pushed off and rode the ladder across the rows of bookshelves to where Frog pointed. He held the ladder while she climbed to the top. Frog signaled when to move the ladder as she searched for the book.

At the very end of the bookshelf, on the very top corner, Frog found it.

Charlie and Frog sat cross-legged on the floor with the book between them. Frog took a deep breath. Charlie did the same.

The answer to what Aggie and Dex and Ray were looking for was inside this book.

Frog reached out her hand. She opened *A Dead Author and Her Secret Treasure*.

# 31. Furious

Blank pages.

The pages in the book were all blank, except for the first page.

*To Sol, keeper of secrets. With love and gratitude, D.J.*

Frog flipped through the book once more. She shook it to see if anything fell out. Nothing did.

*Grandpa Sol?* Frog wrote. *A secret keeper?*

How did any of this make sense?

*Remember what the yearbook said about Aggie?* Charlie wrote.

Frog nodded. *Aggie is a secret teller. Aggie must have told someone about the secret message on D.J.'s headstone, about how to find the book* A Dead Author and Her Secret Treasure.

Charlie thought for a moment.

*WHY is there a secret message on D. J. McKinnon's headstone? And why is THIS book the secret? What's so special about this book?*

*Something that's inside this book*, Frog answered. *But there's nothing inside this book!*

*A secret code written in invisible ink?* Charlie wondered.

*On which page? And even if we had something to make it visible, how do we find it without ruining the book?* Frog looked at the binding. *No Dewey decimal number. This isn't the library's* Dead Author *book. Maybe the secret is only in that one.*

Frog stood and did her pacing-while-twisting-her-pearl-necklace thing. She stopped and studied the shelf from which she had taken *A Dead Author and Her Secret Treasure*. Frog frowned. She went up the ladder and put the book back where she had found it. She pulled it out again and came down.

*Grandpa always keeps his books packed tight together. When he takes out a book he always moves the bookends in to hold the books perfectly straight. But the* Dead Author *book was leaning sideways. There's space for one more book. A book is missing.*

"Your dad?" Charlie asked.

Frog shook her head. *Dad knows how Grandpa keeps his books. We all do! Someone took a book who doesn't know Grandpa keeps his books this way.*

As Charlie thought about this he noticed the computer on Grandpa Sol's desk. He thought about his parents. There wasn't enough time for a letter to be mailed from South Africa, but maybe . . .

*Frog, could you check something for me?*

Frog logged on to the computer. Charlie couldn't believe it. His parents had actually written an e-mail to him.

The study lights flashed, startling them both. It was Oliver, flicking the lights off and on to get their attention.

He marched over to Frog and launched a tirade of signs at her. Frog raised her hands and signed, *"Okay, okay!"*

Oliver turned to Charlie. "Mom is furious!"

Oliver swiped a claw-hand upward in front of his face. *"Furious."* Charlie copied the sign.

*"That!"* Oliver signed. "That is what I am telling you! Frog is in massive trouble," Oliver said. "Mom is mad she disappeared. Millie disappeared for a while, too. And Grandpa is still not home. Frog needs to find Mom and you need to catch the next gondola out of here."

. . .

The sky looked dark and angry, ready to storm again. Charlie leaned his head against the cool glass as the gondola pitched over the water. Charlie couldn't stop thinking about everything he and Frog had just discovered. And he couldn't stop thinking about the e-mail from his mom and dad. Charlie hadn't looked at it yet. Because as long as Charlie hadn't looked at it yet, the e-mail could say whatever Charlie wanted it to say. He crossed his fingers. On both hands.

The rain pattered as Charlie walked, plunked as he ran, and then, just as he reached his grandparents' front door, poured. Charlie sat at the kitchen table and finally unfolded the e-mail Frog had printed out for him. Underneath what his parents had written was a slightly blurry photograph of Mr. and Mrs. Tickler next to a giant golden mole.

> Dear Charlie,
>
> We are sending you a photograph of Mugwump, one of the giant golden moles we have been helping. Doesn't he look pleased we are in South Africa with him? We have had plenty of time for swimming as well. We are most grateful both of us brought an extra bathing suit.
>
> How are your grandparents doing? Have you explored the village? After we

return home to take you to the faraway
boarding school we plan to return to
South Africa. Mugwump has indicated he
would like to see more of us, and three
weeks is simply not enough time.

See you soon!

Your parents (Alistair and Myra Tickler)

Charlie studied the picture. His parents were
grinning, but contrary to what they had written,
Mugwump did not seem pleased. He did not seem like
anything at all. He looked like a furry lump with no eyes
and a pink nose. And he was not golden. He was brown.

Charlie left the letter and the picture of Mugwump
and his parents on the kitchen table. His grandparents
were staring at the television in the living room, watching
people yelling at one another. Charlie stood there, waiting for his grandparents to notice him. He swallowed
hard. He tried to keep his watery eyes wide open.

But it didn't work.

Charlie raced up the stairs to his bedroom, hot tears
leaking down his face. He curled up in the window seat
and stared at the rain pelting the glass.

Why didn't his parents want to be with him? Why
was a giant golden mole more important to them
than Charlie? And he was out of ideas for how to get
his grandparents to care about him and want him to

stay—to be there if Charlie needed them, which he did.

Finally, Charlie went to his dresser and picked up *ASL? You Can!* Charlie wouldn't have anyone to sign with at boarding school. What was the point of learning ASL? He would be leaving soon. Leaving Castle-on-the-Hudson. Leaving Castle School for the Deaf. Leaving Frog and her family.

And he knew he would not be coming back.

A knock; Charlie's door burst open.

It was Yvette—a deck of cards in her hand.

# 32. Cow

"It's not going to work," Charlie said as they sat at the kitchen table. "Grandpa and Grandma Tickler only want to watch television."

"Stop talking and start listening," Yvette said.

They were playing a card game called Kings Corners. A game, Yvette insisted, that Charlie's grandparents would want to keep playing for one simple reason.

"Competition," Yvette said. "Irma and Irving each will want to win. And when one doesn't win, he or she will want to play again in order *to* win. Cards bring out the competitiveness in people. Television, on the other hand, lulls them into bovine numbness."

"Bovine?" Charlie said.

"Cows!" Yvette snapped. She cut the deck of cards neatly with one hand.

"You'll be the rule keeper," Yvette decided, "and you'll change the rules every few games so Irma and Irving will need you to make sure they're playing cards right. I'll teach you. You'll teach your grandparents."

It was an easy game to learn. Four cards were placed around the draw pile: north, south, east, and west, leaving the corners empty for the kings. You put down cards from highest to lowest, alternating red and black cards. If someone played a red ten, the next person could play a black nine. If someone played a black king, the next person could play a red queen. The goal was to get rid of all your cards.

"Yvette, it's not going to work," Charlie said again after they had played several hands. "My parents are coming back to take me to boarding school. Then Grandpa and Grandma can watch all the television they want without me bothering them."

"I've been watching you trying to get Irma and Irving to change," Yvette said. "I didn't think it would work. Then I remembered how much I loved to play cards with my grandparents. And I thought, if a boy like you can believe in people changing, why can't I believe, too?"

"Some things," Charlie said, "are impossible to believe." He started to sign "*impossible*." Then he remembered he didn't need to practice ASL anymore.

Yvette ignored this. She made a pitcher of lemonade and placed homemade peanut butter cookies on a plate. "When I say something will work, it will work. Now go in there and tell your grandparents to come into the kitchen for cookies and cards."

. . .

"Charlie, we can't see the commercial—you're blocking the television," Grandma Tickler said. "This is the one where the cow drives. We love this one, don't we, Irving?"

"Ayuh," Grandpa Tickler said.

"Okay," Charlie said, and he went back into the kitchen.

"Get back out there," Yvette said without turning around from the kitchen sink.

Charlie sighed and went back into the living room. Once again he stood in front of the television.

"Grandma and Grandpa, do you want to play cards? Yvette made peanut butter cookies and lemonade—"

The sky flickered outside the living room window. The television went blank.

"Yvette!" Grandma Tickler hollered. "Lightning hit the antenna again!"

Yvette came out of the kitchen. "I'll call Herman after the storm is over," she said.

"Oh, all right," Grandma Tickler said as thunder crashed outside. "I suppose we can play cards with you, Charlie—we have nothing else better to do. Come on, Irving!"

• • •

The next day was as dark as night. Rain thrummed on the roof. Wind lashed at the trees and rattled the windows.

"This is the stormiest summer we've ever had," Grandma Tickler remarked as Grandpa Tickler dealt the cards. They understood how to play now, but Charlie, under Yvette's watchful eye, made sure to modify, remove, or add rules every few hands.

"You deal five cards, Grandpa, not seven," Charlie said. And then a few hands later he told Grandma Tickler, "Grandma, you deal seven cards to each player."

"But Irving dealt five cards when he was the dealer!"

"That's only for every third deal. It's supposed to be seven cards otherwise," Charlie said.

They kept score on a notepad. Grandma Tickler would win a few hands, and then Grandpa Tickler would take the lead. Yvette was right. They both loved to win.

As he played cards, Charlie realized that Grandpa Sol had to be back by now. And that meant Frog had to know something more about Aggie and her secret.

But the gondola wouldn't operate in this weather, so that meant no letter from Frog. And that meant Charlie could only worry and wait.

To distract himself, Charlie talked as he played cards. And as he talked, Charlie realized his grandparents weren't listening to him—had never really listened to him—not even when Charlie talked about listening.

"There was this grave," Charlie remarked as he played a two of diamonds, "that I saw up at the castle."

"Irving, it's your turn—pay attention!"

"On the headstone it said, 'No one ever listens until it's too late.'"

Grandpa Tickler put down an ace of clubs.

"Another grave," Charlie continued, "mentioned a special kind of listening."

"Really, Irving? An ace of clubs?"

"It's not listening with our ears," Charlie said.

"Ayuh!"

"And it's not listening with our eyes."

"Don't tell me to be quiet, Irving!"

"And it's not listening with our hands, like how Obie the caretaker listens. Instead, we have to listen with something else."

Grandpa Tickler lifted his gaze and looked at Charlie, almost as if waiting for Charlie to tell him what that something else was.

• • •

The next morning, the day of the Founders' Day Dinner, the rain stopped. Herman stepped out of the taxi and strapped on the harness. Charlie stood outside and watched. Herman gripped the edges of the ladder. He placed one foot on the first step, braced himself, and then pulled the other foot up. He paused and took a breath. Charlie counted one-Mississippi, two-Mississippi, three-Mississippi. Then Herman placed a foot on the second rung. He braced, then (one-Mississippi, two-Mississippi, three-Mississippi) pulled himself up.

Charlie went inside. Grandma and Grandpa Tickler sat in their E-Z chair recliners, waiting for the TV to turn on again. Once the television was fixed, Grandma and Grandpa Tickler wouldn't need Charlie anymore.

What had Yvette called it?

Bovine numbness . . . bovine . . . cow.

Charlie went upstairs. He opened his *ASL? You Can!* book to the sign for "cow."

Charlie signed the letter *Y*, touched his thumb to the side of his temple, and twisted his wrist forward twice. Then he remembered again—he didn't need to practice ASL anymore. He slammed the book shut.

Charlie needed to get to the castle. He needed to find Aggie.

# 33. Secret

Grandpa Sol was still gone. And Frog was still without a key to the library.

Mrs. Castle was ordering this, commanding that, directing this, arranging that.

*She hasn't showered in two days!* Frog wrote. *That's the only time she is away from her keys!*

They needed to find a real copy of *A Dead Author and Her Secret Treasure*, not one with just blank pages—and the school library was their last hope.

But Frog did have something to show Charlie. A Founders' Day Dinner name tag. *Agatha Penderwick, CSD Alum.*

*That means Aggie IS coming!* Charlie wrote.

*IF she makes it,* Frog replied.

*What does that mean?*

*I mean this is a murder mystery! Dex and Ray are still out there.*

Charlie thought about *Vince Vinelli's Worst Criminals Ever!*

*Aren't you worried something might have happened to Grandpa Sol?*

*Don't say that! Grandpa is fine!*

But underneath her diamond tiara, Frog's eyes looked worried. Charlie wished he hadn't said anything.

• • •

Charlie pulled weeds, polished silver, swept and mopped floors. He was cleaning the glass on a display case when Frog pointed to her mother going up the stairs.

*Mom is getting ready to shower,* Frog wrote. *I'm going to get the library key off her key ring.*

This seemed dangerous. If Frog's mother caught her...

But five minutes later Frog was at the top of the staircase, the library key in her palm. Oliver threw down his polishing cloth and followed Charlie.

"This is sure to end badly," Oliver told Charlie as they took the stairs two at a time. "And yet, I can't help myself."

They raced up the second set of stairs that led to the library tower. Frog inserted the key and the door swung open. Charlie and Oliver followed her up twisty stairs that spilled into a bright, round room lined with books.

After all their searching, the school library had seemed like a last-ditch effort. One final attempt to find the book that Aggie and Dex and Ray had been looking for. The book that held Aggie's secret.

Charlie hadn't really expected to find anything.

But, unbelievably, there it was.

A crumpled sleeping bag, a plate of half-eaten peanut-butter-and-jelly sandwiches, and the book *A Dead Author and Her Secret Treasure* by D. J. McKinnon. A Dewey decimal number marked its binding: **419.7** REF.

Frog picked up the book, took a deep breath, and opened it.

Blank pages. Again. Just like the copy in Grandpa Sol's study. But these blank pages had been cut into a rectangle-shaped hole. In the empty space was a folded note.

> *D.J.*
> *The treasure inside this book is being restored to its former glory.*
> *I promise it will be returned soon.*
> *S.C.*

Solomon Castle. Why would Grandpa Sol write a note to a dead person?

Charlie heard footsteps on the library stairs. Bear bounded into the library followed by Millie.

*"No!"* Millie signed with both hands. *"No, no, no!"* She stamped her foot. Millie's hands were a blur as she signed to Frog and Oliver, who signed back to her and to each other. All those hands talking at the same time was making Charlie dizzy.

Finally Millie turned to him. "You aren't supposed to be in here, Charlie! I promised Aggie when I helped her hide in here! It's supposed to be a secret!" Millie signed the letter *A*, and tapped the back of her thumb against her lips twice. *"Secret."* Charlie automatically copied the sign.

*"A secret? You have to tell us what's going on, Millie,"* Frog signed as Oliver interpreted for Charlie. *"Why did you help Aggie hide up here? And how did you know there was a secret key to the library?"*

*"James told me,"* Millie said. *"He wanted to make sure I could get books from the library while he was gone."*

*"James shouldn't have told you,"* Frog said. *"You can't keep a secret."*

*"I can too keep a secret!"* Millie said. *"It's Aggie who can't!"* Millie stuck out her bottom lip. *"Aggie told a secret she wasn't supposed to tell. That's why she was trying to find a book before two men found it. She finally found it*

*in Grandpa's study. But what was supposed to be inside the book was gone. Then Aggie read the note Grandpa left. Aggie said she knew where to look next."*

*"Where?"* Frog asked.

Millie shook her head.

*"We're trying to help Aggie,"* Frog said. *"You have to tell us!"*

Millie looked from Frog to Oliver to Charlie. Finally she signed something.

"The Naked You?" Oliver said. "Why would she go there?"

The Naked You? What was that?

Before Charlie could ask, he heard a loud shout. Bear sprang up and ran down the library stairs.

*"What?"* Frog signed.

*"Mom,"* Oliver told her.

Frog looked at the key in her hand. It was too late to put it back on the key ring.

They locked up the library and followed Bear to the top of the stairs overlooking the great hall. Frog's mom, wearing a bathrobe and a towel around her hair, was hugging a white-haired man with a bandaged ankle, leaning on a pair of tree-branch crutches.

Grandpa Sol was home.

# 34. Trouble

Frog, Oliver, and Millie ran down the stairs. Charlie slowly followed, feeling like an outsider as they clung to Grandpa Sol and his backpack like koalas to a tree.

Were koalas endangered?

Would his parents be helping koalas next?

Then Frog, Oliver, and Millie were all signing at once, trying to be seen by Grandpa Sol to get his attention. Frog's mother silenced them so she could yell at Grandpa Sol. In his mind Charlie interpreted.

*"Where have you been? You were supposed to have been home days ago! What have you done to your foot? The*

*Founders' Day Dinner is today and you haven't even writ-ten your speech and you are filthy and you need a shower!"* And so on.

Finally Mrs. Castle stopped signing and pointed upstairs with a sweep of her arm. Grandpa Sol obeyed. He hobbled up the stairs with the help of Mr. Castle, Frog's mother right behind them.

"Grandpa Sol has to clean up and get his speech written," Oliver said to Charlie, who was pleased he had understood. "No one is allowed to talk to him until then," Oliver added.

*"We have to go bring Aggie here,"* Frog told Charlie as Oliver interpreted. *"We have to bring her back to Grandpa. If we go now, we can be back before the celebration starts."*

"But Aggie is coming here," Charlie said. "We saw her name tag!"

*"Not if Dex and Ray get to her first,"* Frog said.

*"How do you sign 'TROUBLE'?"* Charlie asked Frog.

Frog signed the letter *B* with both hands near the side of her head. She quickly crossed and opened them in front of her face several times. *"Trouble."*

*"You will be in so much trouble,"* Charlie told her.

*"True that,"* Oliver said.

*"But,"* Charlie signed, using what he learned from his ASL book, *"good people do good things."*

• • •

It would have been madness for them all to go. Oliver wanted to come for protection, but Millie insisted she and Bear were going if Oliver was. In the end Oliver said it was up to him to be the voice of reason and stay. Millie would help Oliver distract anyone searching for Frog while they were gone.

Charlie and Frog bolted for the gondola. Charlie learned that their destination was actually the Naked *Ewe*, a knitting shop owned by Miss Tweedy's sister, Enid. "Ewe" and "you" sounded the same in English, but they looked nothing alike in ASL. As they crossed the river, Frog scrawled a note to Chief Paley.

Charlie handed Mr. Simple five dollars when they reached the other side. "Mr. Simple, would you deliver this letter to Chief Paley right away? It's important!"

Mr. Simple counted the bills. "You betcha."

"When does the gondola leave next?" Charlie asked.

Mr. Simple looked at his watch and signed three threes.

Three thirty-three? Charlie looked at his watch and showed it to Frog. They had seventeen minutes to get to the Naked Ewe and back.

• • •

Charlie and Frog raced to the Naked Ewe. When they reached the yellow Victorian house, they paused

to catch their breath. Charlie looked at his watch—
fourteen minutes left. Quietly they climbed the steps on
the side of the big front porch. Dropping to their hands
and knees, they crawled to the front windows. Slowly
Charlie and Frog raised their heads and peered inside.

Charlie saw shelves of colorful yarn, knitted sweat-
ers and scarves on display . . . and tiny Aggie staring at
someone, hands on her wrinkled cheeks. Next to Aggie
was a woman who looked like Miss Tweedy, armed with
a knitting needle. This must be Enid, Miss Tweedy's
sister.

Charlie moved his head just enough to see who
Aggie and Enid were facing.

There stood Dex and Ray.

Charlie and Frog crouched back down and gave each
other a look. Both knew what had to be done.

Charlie pulled out his key. Frog pulled off her diamond tiara and held it with the sharp prongs facing
out.

Charlie and Frog flung open the front door just as
Enid shouted, "Aggie's not going anywhere with you!
Frog? *Frog! Get the police!*" Enid almost stabbed herself
with the knitting needle as she signed *"police."*

Charlie and Frog edged into the shop with their
knuckles straight out in front of them.

"What's all this?" Dex asked.

"It's those kids, Dex."

"Yeah, I see that. Look, lady"—Dex turned to Enid—"there's no need for the police. We just want to talk with Aggie."

Dex signed to Aggie, who shook her head and signed, *"No!"*

"She already told you she doesn't want to talk. She's not going to tell you anything!" Enid said.

Dex signed to Aggie.

"What did you say?" Ray asked.

"I told her we can split whatever is inside the book," Dex said.

"Aggie already told you—what's inside the book isn't for stealing!" Enid said. "It's for everyone to share."

Aggie folded her arms and glared at Dex and Ray. Her confidence had grown since Charlie and Frog had arrived. She now looked a bit like Dorrie McCann on the cover of *Dorrie McCann and the Mystery of the Secret Treasure*.

Charlie and Frog moved next to Aggie and Enid. They faced Dex and Ray armed with a knitting needle, a diamond tiara, and a house key.

"I'm real scared," Dex said. "What are you going to do? Knit, crown, or key us?"

"Are you being serious, Dex? Because all those things could really hurt."

"They're not going to hurt," Dex said, "because we're going to—"

"Nobody move!" Chief Paley shouted as she and Miss Tweedy burst through the door.

"Enid, are you all right?" Miss Tweedy rushed over to her. "Walter Simple told me the chief was needed at the Naked Ewe and— Oh my goodness, Enid, what's going on?"

Charlie sighed with relief and lowered his hand. Frog continued to hold her tiara, ready to stab Dex in the eye. Charlie tapped her arm. Frog dropped her hand and grinned at Charlie.

Everyone was signing and talking to Chief Paley at the same time. Charlie looked at his watch.

"Chief Paley!" Charlie said. "We have to catch the next gondola! The Founders' Day Dinner is about to start!"

"We need to get going, too," Dex said.

"Yeah," Ray agreed.

"You two aren't going anywhere until I know if a crime has been committed," Chief Paley said. "Charlie and Frog, you two go. Enid and Aggie can tell me what's going on."

Charlie and Frog had unanswered questions that would have to wait. They had three minutes to catch the gondola.

Aggie signed something fast to Charlie and Frog. Frog nodded but Charlie didn't understand. So Enid spoke into English what Aggie had signed.

*"Watch out for Tony!"*

# 35. Nice to Meet You

"Shirt," Oliver ordered, handing Charlie the Castle School for the Deaf shirt he had just ironed. "Deodorant." Oliver threw a bottle on the bed as Charlie pulled off his sweaty T-shirt.

"Deodorant? I'm ten!"

"Deodorant doesn't care that you're ten. Deodorant cares that you're smelly. Look, I have to help in the kitchen. Afterward you and Frog need to tell me everything, all right?"

Oliver hurried out of the room.

Charlie splashed water on his face and combed down his hair. His cowlick ignored the comb. Charlie thought about Aggie. He and Frog still hadn't learned what Aggie had been looking for in the book *A Dead Author and Her Secret Treasure.*

Why had Aggie thought it would be at the Naked Ewe?

Who was Tony?

And why did they have to watch out for him?

Charlie dabbed cold deodorant under his arms and pulled on his iron-warmed shirt. Frog came out of her bedroom wearing her tiara *and* long earrings, a longer necklace, six bracelets, her emerald ring, and Aggie's red flower. It was, after all, a special day.

Mr. Castle paced by the front doors, waiting for the first guests to arrive. Mrs. Castle stood over Grandpa as he sat in a chair and finished writing his speech, his bandaged ankle elevated. Charlie and Frog watched wide-eyed from their station at the name-tag table.

People trickled into the castle. Then they streamed and then gushed. More and more people arrived for the Founders' Day Dinner to celebrate the place they called home. The air was a whirlwind of hands and arms and hugs. More hugs than Charlie had ever seen before. Bear's tail never stopped wagging.

Alumni came over to get their name tags. They oohed and aahed over Frog, how big she was, how beautiful she looked in her tiara and jewelry.

Frog had taught Charlie how to sign "*nice to meet*

*you.*" Charlie was busy sliding one palm over the other palm, signing the number *1* with both hands, touching them knuckle to knuckle, and then pointing to each person he met. "*Nice to meet you.*"

Charlie and Frog handed out name tag after name tag. Charlie searched the entire time for one that said "Tony."

A man came up and spelled his name. JERRY LEVY. Frog looked for his name tag, but couldn't find it. The man corrected himself and fingerspelled another name. Frog found the name tag with "Gerald Levy" on it, and handed it to him.

Frog explained. *Jerry was his nickname,* Frog wrote.

Charlie thought about what Frog had just written: Jerry was his nickname.

Like Frog was a nickname for Francine.

Charlie had been looking for a name tag with "Tony" on it. But if Tony was also a nickname . . . Charlie grabbed his notebook and pen.

*We should be looking for a name tag with "Anthony" on it!* Charlie wrote.

Frog gave Charlie a puzzled look. She reached for the notebook and pen.

*But Anthony is a man's name,* Frog told him.

*Right,* Charlie replied. *But Tony is a man's name. And Tony is a nickname for Anthony.*

Frog shook her head. *Aggie didn't sign, "Watch out*

for T-O-N-Y." *Aggie signed, "Watch out for T-O-N-I."*

Enid had interpreted what Aggie had signed for Charlie. So Charlie only *heard* what Aggie had signed. But Frog *saw* what Aggie had signed. When you hear the names "Tony" and "Toni," they sound the same. When you see the names "Tony" and "Toni," they look different.

Frog continued writing. *But you're right! Toni is probably a nickname for a woman named—*

Just then a silver-haired woman wearing huge diamond earrings approached the table. It was the same woman Charlie and Frog had seen in Junk and Stuff. The woman fingerspelled her name. Frog gave Charlie a sidelong glance before she found the woman's name tag: Antoinette Penny.

Antoinette Penny turned away without even a thank-you. Frog grabbed Charlie's arm.

*Toni is a nickname for Antoinette! That has to be her!*

*Are you sure?* Charlie was doubtful. *I mean she was rude, but she doesn't look like someone—*

*Like someone to watch out for?* Frog finished his sentence. *Just because you LOOK good doesn't mean you ARE good. Even if her diamond earrings are amazing. Besides,* Frog added, *I looked into her eyes—her eyes were NOT good!*

Charlie and Frog watched Toni mingle in the great hall as they continued to hand out name tags.

Finally Grandpa Sol called the crowd together, ready to give his welcoming speech. Two men helped him climb the stairs to a chair on the stage that had been set up.

"Can everyone please find a seat? We're about to begin." As Grandpa signed, a man spoke into a microphone, interpreting for those who were sign-impaired.

People shuffled around, looking for their seats.

A woman approached Toni and gestured to a chair. Frog stood on her tiptoes to catch the conversation.

*Toni said her back hurts,* Frog told Charlie. *She said she prefers to stand. I don't believe her!*

But Toni didn't just stand. Toni was slowly edging out of the great hall.

*Where's she going?* Charlie asked.

*I don't know.* Frog watched Toni as she moved along the wall. *But we're going to find out!*

Toni glided past the Flying Hands Café and out the front door.

• • •

Charlie and Frog trailed Toni as she circled around the castle and slipped inside the back entrance. They waited a minute. Then they followed Toni inside, through hallways, and up the narrow back stairs.

A light turned on.

Toni was in Grandpa Sol's study.

Charlie and Frog watched her through the slightly cracked-open door.

Toni was scanning the bookshelves.

*She's looking for the* Dead Author *book!* Frog wrote.

Charlie could hear snatches of Grandpa's words being interpreted into English downstairs: *"Our school . . . home for Deaf children . . . in their natural language."*

Toni bent down, hands on her knees, and studied books on the bottom shelves. Suddenly she straightened and turned around. Charlie and Frog jerked away from the door. They waited, hearts pounding, ready to run.

Nothing happened.

They inched forward to peer through the crack again.

Toni's head was tilted back as she searched the top shelves. She moved the ladder over and began to climb. She climbed really well for someone old. She was right in the middle of the alumni book section.

*She's going to steal the book!* Frog wrote. *She must not know it's blank inside. Thief!*

*How do you sign "thief"?* Charlie asked.

*You'll see!*

*"We will continue . . . help our children . . . find their power within . . ."* Grandpa's words echoed in Charlie's ears.

Charlie and Frog watched Toni reach for *A Dead Author and Her Secret Treasure*. She tucked it in the bag hanging on her shoulder, and then climbed down with both hands.

Frog flew into the room with her diamond tiara pointed outward. Charlie followed with his key.

*"Thief!"* Frog yelled in ASL. *"That book is not yours!"*

Toni reeled back. She gripped the edge of a chair to steady herself. She glared at Charlie and Frog.

Frog was right. Toni did not have good eyes.

Toni clutched her bag and shouldered past them out the study door. Toni was getting away—but Charlie's key and Frog's tiara were only for protection. To catch Toni they needed help.

Charlie and Frog ran toward the top of the stairs of the great hall. What does Vince Vinelli say to yell when a crime is being committed? Fire! But yelling fire when there is no fire in a crowded hall would not be very sensible. So instead:

*"Help! Thief!"* Frog yelled in ASL.

"Help! Thief!" Charlie yelled in English.

Grandpa stopped his speech as the crowd buzzed. *"What? Where?"* they signed.

*"What's going on?"* Grandpa Sol signed to Frog as people hurried up the stairs toward them.

Just then Chief Paley strode through the front entrance of the great hall. She held Toni by the arm as Aggie followed behind them, the *Dead Author* book lifted high in the air.

# 36. Pah!

The Founders' Day Dinner had been a smashing success. When it was over, Frog's family gathered in their apartment, along with Charlie, Chief Paley, and Aggie. The interpreter from the celebration joined them so that everyone could understand each other.

"I'm so glad you're here," Oliver told the interpreter, "because I need a break."

Mrs. Castle signed first.

"*I want to know what happened,*" Mrs. Castle said. "*Now.*"

"*Be calm, dear,*" Mr. Castle said.

"*Don't tell me to be calm!*"

"*Charlie, why don't you start,*" Grandpa Sol said before Mrs. Castle could say anything else.

"Well," Charlie said as the interpreter signed. "It all began the day I went to the library and met Aggie—"

But Aggie was bursting to tell the story.

"*I told a secret!*" Aggie said. "*Again! This time I had to make it right before it was too late.*"

"*That story my dad told us,*" Frog said, "*that was you! You're the one who told the secret about the manuscript D. J. McKinnon was writing. And I bet Toni was the person you told. And Toni was the one who burned it!*"

"*The frenemy!*" Oliver said.

"*It was Toni.*" Aggie nodded. "*D.J. forgave me for telling her secret—but she also forgave Toni for burning it! I couldn't believe it. How does someone forgive something so awful? But D.J. did—she said she didn't want hate in her heart. But not me.*" Aggie shook her head fiercely. "*I couldn't forgive Toni. But then, last week, Toni called me. She said she wanted to put what had happened behind us, before another Founders' Day Dinner went by.*"

"But why now?" Charlie asked. "After all this time?"

"*People can change,*" Grandpa Sol said. "*Maybe she really did want to make amends.*"

"*I never gave her a chance,*" Aggie said. "*I told Toni I would never forgive her. I told her D.J. had hidden a secret*" *treasure that only people who truly loved her would be able to find—so she never would. I said it to be mean. I said it to hurt Toni."*

"*When planning revenge . . .*" Oliver began.

"*. . . be prepared to dig two graves,*" Chief Paley finished.

Aggie sighed. "*That is so true. Because when I saw Toni's nephew, Dex, on the phone behind her, I knew I was in trouble. I knew Toni would send someone like him to look for it. I came as fast as I could to the village. But the book was gone. And Sol was gone, too!*"

"*Bear and I helped Aggie while she waited for Grandpa and tried to find the book herself!*" Millie said. "*See, I can keep a secret!*"

"*Sometimes,*" Oliver agreed.

"*All the time!*" Millie said. Bear barked in agreement.

"*Enough,*" Mrs. Castle said.

"*Listen to your mother,*" Mr. Castle said.

"*You know I go on my hike every year, Aggie,*" Grandpa Sol said.

"*And next year you're taking a cell phone with you,*" Mrs. Castle said. "*No arguing.*"

"*Aggie, what was in the book?*" Frog signed what Charlie had been thinking.

"*That's where I come in,*" Grandpa Sol said. "*When D.J. knew she was dying, she asked me to help her plan her last mystery—a final gift to her readers. I made sure her headstone was inscribed the way she wanted. Harold Woo shelved the special book she had made in the village library."*

"*You never told me!*" Frog said.

"*The fun is figuring it out,*" Grandpa Sol said. "*And I knew you would eventually. But what was hidden inside the book needed cleaning and repair. Miss Tweedy would not have approved of D.J.'s secret book and its special Dewey decimal number. I tried to talk to Miss Tweedy about it when she became acting librarian. I worried she might get rid of the book now that Harold Woo was not there. But I couldn't talk to her because she was still too upset about Harold dying so suddenly.*"

"Plus she hates anything with the word 'dead' in it," Charlie added.

"*So true!*" Grandpa Sol said. "*I decided to wait until I could return the book and the treasure inside of it, and then explain everything to Miss Tweedy. I had planned to be home before any alumni arrived. I didn't plan, however, to step in that hole and twist my ankle.*"

"What treasure?!" Charlie asked.

"*What treasure?!*" Frog signed.

Aggie pulled out the library book *A Dead Author and Her Secret Treasure* from her large purse. She handed the book to Charlie and Frog.

Together they opened it.

Frog gasped.

Inside the book was a red scarf. Not Aggie's red scarf—a different red scarf.

Charlie held the book while Frog lifted the scarf out with both hands. She nestled it to her cheek. She breathed in deeply. Finally Frog raised her head and looked at Grandpa Sol.

*"Yes."* Grandpa Sol nodded. *"That scarf belonged to D. J. McKinnon."*

A huge smile lit up Frog's face. Eyes shining, she hugged the red scarf before wrapping it around her neck.

*"She wrote all of her books wearing it!"* Frog said.

"She even had Dorrie McCann wear a red scarf whenever she needed to believe in herself," Charlie added as the interpreter signed.

*"D.J. wanted her readers to feel the same way about their own power,"* Grandpa Sol said.

*"So she hid the scarf and left a clue on her headstone how to find it,"* Frog said.

*"Exactly,"* Grandpa Sol said. *"Fans who have found it kept it a secret, so each person could find it in his or her own time. Harold Woo watched over the book and scarf. Fans who deciphered the code would come to the library, find the book, and wear the scarf. They would spend a few moments feeling their own power with the memory of their beloved author. That's why the scarf needed to be cleaned and repaired by Enid. It was worn-out because of love."*

"*What happened to those two men?*" Mrs. Castle asked Chief Paley. "*The ones who tried to steal the scarf?*"

"Well," Chief Paley said, "Dex and Ray were vexed—no, that's not the right word." The chief thought for a moment. "Dex and Ray were infuriated when they found out the treasure they had been hunting for turned out to be just a scarf. I told them one man's trash is another man's treasure—"

"*D.J.'s scarf isn't trash!*" Frog said.

"*It's called a metaphor,*" Oliver said. "*Calm down.*"

"I informed Dex and Ray," the chief continued, "that it was in the best interest of our village that they leave town and not come back—ever."

"But what about Toni?" Charlie asked. "Toni stole a book!"

"*I told Chief Paley I wouldn't press any charges,*" Grandpa Sol said. "*Toni has to live with herself.*"

"*Grandpa, why did you leave a note to D.J. inside the book?*" Frog asked.

"*That was me talking to my friend,*" Grandpa Sol said. "*I miss her. I wanted her to know I was still keeping her secret safe and would have it back again soon.*"

"Why did you have a blank copy of D.J.'s *Dead Author* book in your study?" Charlie asked.

"*That was D.J. and her sense of humor. She knew I like to have a copy of every book written by alumni. So she made* two copies of her book. In one book she hollowed out the pages, and hid her scarf inside of it. The other copy she gave to me."

"I miss her, too," Aggie said. "She was the kindest person I ever knew."

"And the most amazing writer," Frog said.

"Her book was pretty good," Charlie said.

"You mean great," Frog signed.

"True that," Chief Paley agreed.

"That's why I needed to make sure her scarf was safe," Aggie said. "Thank you, Charlie and Frog. Thank you for caring about me. Thank you, thank you, thank you!" Aggie repeated the first sign Charlie had ever learned.

"You're welcome," Charlie and Frog signed.

"And me and Bear!" Millie said. "We helped!"

"And Millie and Bear!" Aggie hugged them both. "You make the best peanut-butter-and-jelly sandwiches!"

Frog unpinned the red flower from her shirt.

"Here, Aggie," Frog said. "This is yours. Charlie and I found it at D.J.'s grave. We didn't know if you had left it on purpose."

"I did leave it on purpose," Aggie said. "I made it for D.J. years ago. She gave it back to me before she died. But now it's yours to keep."

"Really?" Frog's smile, if it was possible, stretched even bigger. "Thank you! But wait—what about Charlie? He found it, too!" Frog turned to him. "I know! We'll share the flower, fifty-fifty! I'll wear it Mondays, you can wear it Tuesdays—"

"I'm good," Charlie said as the interpreter signed. "You can wear it for both of us."

*"You're sure?"*

"Definitely," Charlie said. "And Aggie, you dropped this."

Charlie handed Aggie her knitting bag.

*"Thank you!"* Aggie said again. She reached inside her bag and pulled out her own half-knitted red scarf. *"Now I can finish this and have my own scarf to remind me that I have power—power to make different choices."*

*"To forgive Toni perhaps?"* Grandpa Sol suggested.

*"Don't push it,"* Aggie signed. *"But you never know. People can change. Even me."*

Grandpa engulfed tiny Aggie in a big hug.

*Pah!* Frog wrote.

*Pah?* Charlie asked. *What's that mean?*

*Pah! It means we did it!*

Frog placed both index fingers near the sides of her chin, palms facing inward. Then she turned her hands forward and up as her lips popped open. *"We did it. Pah!"*

Charlie made the sign for himself. *"Pah!"*

*We solved a murder mystery!* Frog wrote.

*But without the murder part,* Charlie added.

For a moment Frog looked disappointed. Then she wrote: *Murder mysteries without the murder are probably the best kind of murder mysteries.*

*But you can still put it on your résumé,* Charlie told her.

*I will!* Frog wrote. *It's my first real investigation!*

"*That,*" Charlie signed. That is exactly right.

Charlie told himself it was a good thing that Aggie was fine and D.J.'s secret had been protected. So why did Charlie feel sad now that the murder-mystery-without-the-murder was over?

He looked around at the Castle family and Aggie and Chief Paley, all signing and laughing and arguing and caring about each other.

And he knew why he felt sad.

Charlie asked Millie for a turn wearing D. J. McKinnon's hidden treasure. He carefully wound the soft scarf around his neck, closed his eyes, and took a few deep breaths. The sounds of sign language surrounded him. The scarf smelled of lemon and lavender.

Charlie thought about the power that was inside of him. Then he stopped thinking and just felt—he felt that power deep within.

He needed that power now to ask for what he wanted.

Charlie asked to speak to Grandpa Sol in private.

# 37. Missed You

Chief Paley rode the gondola with Charlie back to the village, and then walked him back to his grandparents' house. To Charlie's surprise, his grandparents were waiting for him. The television was turned off. Cards were laid out on the kitchen table, ready to be played.

"You're back!" Grandma Tickler said. "Finally! We said, 'Where did Charlie go?' And then I said, 'We should know where Charlie went.' Didn't I say that, Irving?"

"Ayuh," Grandpa Tickler said.

"I guess Herman couldn't fix the antenna," Charlie said.

"He fixed it all right," Grandma Tickler said, "and he fell off the roof, too. Twice! Good thing we had that harness on him."

"If he fixed it, then why aren't you watching TV?" Charlie asked.

"We wanted to play cards," Grandma Tickler said, "with you! We missed you, Charlie! Didn't we miss him, Irving?"

"You did?" Charlie said. "Really?"

"Ayuh," Grandpa Tickler said.

"Aw, Charlie!" Chief Paley thumped Charlie on the back—hard. "Do you want to know how to say that in sign language?" Chief Paley touched the tip of her index finger to the middle of her chin, and then pointed at Charlie. "*Missed you.*"

And Charlie, as always, copied the sign so he would not forget it.

Yvette gave a satisfied nod.

"Is that Kings Corners?" Chief Paley asked. "I love Kings Corners! My grandma always played with me!" The chief extended her hand to Grandma Tickler. "Chief of Police Augusta Paley. How do you do?"

"Chief Paley?" Grandma Tickler said. "We had Herman drive us to the police station, but it was closed. We were worried about Aggie Penderwick!"

"I apologize for the inconvenience, ma'am," Chief Paley said. "As for Aggie Penderwick, Charlie and Frog helped her. If you let me join your game, I'll tell you what I know."

Yvette and Chief Paley both sat down. Charlie dealt everyone a hand of cards.

"Only five cards?" Chief Paley asked. "I thought you're supposed to deal seven."

"Aren't the rules confusing?" Grandma Tickler said. "It's a good thing we have Charlie around. He knows all the rules."

As they played Kings Corners, the chief told the story of Aggie. Chief Paley spoke of libraries and books and knitting. She told of a secret treasure that was supposed to stay a secret. She spun a tale of a woman trying to right her wrongdoing, and protect the treasure. Even Charlie was riveted.

"Charlie and Frog," Chief Paley concluded, "followed Vince Vinelli's motto."

"Good people do good things!" Grandma Tickler said. "Chief Paley, did you know we taught Charlie everything he knows about self-defense? Irving, get up. Let's show her!"

"Here we go," Yvette said, as Grandma and Grandpa Tickler got out of their chairs.

They faced each other and bowed. Grandpa Tickler threw a wobbly round punch. It was a slow enough punch that Grandma Tickler had time to block it with her forearm, even though she was moving at the speed of mud. Grandpa Tickler sliced air with a steady vengeance. Grandma Tickler waited for him to finish, then she flicked a few tiny kicks in his vicinity.

Charlie's crime-fighting grandparents were back.

Chief Paley fist-bumped Grandma and Grandpa Tickler. Then they resumed playing cards. Grandma Tickler won the round and gloated.

For the next game Charlie dealt seven cards to each player. "If you stop playing and then start again," Charlie explained, "it's always seven cards next time."

"That's right," Yvette agreed as they started to play.

When it was his turn, Charlie played the king of hearts. He placed it in an empty corner.

"Cards are so much fun," Grandma Tickler said. "Charlie has the best ideas. We should listen to him more often, shouldn't we, Irving?"

Grandpa Tickler did not respond.

"Irving! It's your turn!"

But Grandpa Tickler was staring at the card Charlie had just played. He touched it with his finger.

"Irving?"

Grandpa Tickler lifted his gaze and looked at Charlie. He cleared his throat.

"Hearts," Grandpa Tickler said softly, to Charlie's surprise. "We can listen with our hearts."

Someone had heard Charlie after all.

"Ayuh," Charlie said.

# 38. I'm Here If You Need Me

Eleven days later Charlie helped his parents bring in their luggage from Herman's taxi.

"We want Charlie to stay with us," Grandma Tickler said as soon as Charlie's parents walked in the house. "Charlie taught us the most marvelous card game—Kings Corners!"

"If you like Kings Corners, Grandma," Charlie said, "then you're going to love a new game I just learned. It's called Spite and Malice."

"Ooooh," Grandma Tickler said. "I like the sound of that!"

Yvette winked as Charlie's parents turned to him in surprise.

"You bonded!" Mrs. Tickler said. "Well done, Charlie! We didn't think you would!"

"Bonding is so important," Mr. Tickler said. "We learned that with Mugwump. Now, Charlie, about that hundred-dollar bill and my change—?"

Charlie put down the last suitcase and turned to his father.

"Dad, did you know I'm an endangered animal?" Charlie asked. "Just like Mugwump. Because there's only one of me in the entire world."

"Ayuh," Grandpa Tickler said.

Charlie's parents thought about this.

It was a new thought.

One that had never occurred to them.

• • •

That first night back, as Charlie's parents were getting ready for bed, Charlie stopped them.

"You can't go to bed yet," Charlie said. "First you have to tuck me in."

Tucking in was a new concept for Charlie's parents. They had no idea how to do it. Charlie was going to have to teach them.

Charlie showed them how to check the closet and under the bed to make sure he was safe. Bring him a glass of water. Ask him if he had brushed his teeth.

"But you always brush your teeth," Mrs. Tickler said.

"You still have to ask me," Charlie said. "Then you pull up my blanket and kiss me good night. You tell me I must go to sleep, but I'll be taking out a flashlight and reading anyway."

"Pull up blanket, kiss, tell him go to sleep, will ignore parents and read regardless." Mr. Tickler wrote down Charlie's instructions so they wouldn't forget. "Is that everything?"

No, it wasn't everything.

As his parents prepared to leave his bedroom, Charlie said, "Wait."

He still couldn't tell his parents the last thing he wanted. But he could show them in sign. Charlie held up his hand with his two middle fingers folded, and his thumb, forefinger, and pinky extended. The sign Mrs. Castle had used when she had tucked him in.

"I remember using that sign as a child," Mr. Tickler said. "But I seem to have forgotten what it means."

# 39. Friends

Charlie paced on the front porch, waiting. And worrying.

Yvette poked her head out the window. "Quit your worrying! Everything is going to be fine!"

Charlie stopped pacing. "Really, Yvette? You really think so?"

"Yes, I really think so," Yvette said. "Eleanor Castle—Frog's mother? She is one fierce woman. She'll make it happen."

Charlie crossed his fingers.

"I told Irma and Irving you can ride the gondola back and forth every day and still be with them," Yvette said.

"And I made sure Alistair and Myra know it's cheaper than that boarding school. Now I have to go check on my cake. We're going to need it to celebrate—you'll see!"

Charlie continued to pace, waiting for Mr. Simple to bring the most important letter of all.

But it wasn't Mr. Simple who walked up the street.

It was Frog. She climbed the porch steps and handed Charlie the letter he had been waiting for.

Charlie tried to read her face, but Frog, for the first time since Charlie had known her, was expressionless.

They sat down side by side on the top step. Charlie glanced over his shoulder. Yvette was watching through the window, wringing a kitchen towel.

Charlie opened the envelope. Frog leaned closer to Charlie.

Grandpa Sol had written Charlie a one-word answer. *Yes*.

Yes, Charlie would be allowed to attend Castle School for the Deaf.

"*Wow*," Charlie signed.

Frog jumped up and twirled around, her long sapphire necklace swinging with her.

Charlie stared at the letter, not believing it was true.

But it *was* true.

Yvette opened the window. "Told you so! We're going to celebrate tonight!" She slammed the window shut.

Frog plopped down next to Charlie and opened her notebook. *Mom told Grandpa Sol you have to come to our school. Even though you are hearing and not a Castle.*

"*Why?*" Charlie signed. "*Why me?*"

*Because,* Frog told Charlie, *Mom said you need us.*

Charlie felt his eyes fill up. He tried to keep them wide open. But, of course, that doesn't always work. He tried to wipe his eyes without Frog noticing.

Frog continued writing as if she hadn't noticed, even though Charlie knew she had.

*Mom can tutor you in ASL, and Dad can tutor you in your other subjects until you learn enough ASL to under-stand the teachers. Now you HAVE to practice!*

Charlie gave a final wipe of his eyes with the back of his hand.

"*I will!*" Charlie signed. *But,* he wrote, *you have to be patient! Like you are with Miss Tweedy.*

*I'M ALWAYS PATIENT!!!*

Charlie gave Frog his best Frog look.

"*What?!*"

Charlie tried to raise one eyebrow. He couldn't, so he narrowed his eyes instead.

Frog sighed dramatically. *OKAY! I'll try to be more patient.*

*You better!* Charlie told her.

Frog looked at Charlie for a long moment. *I have to be patient,* she finally wrote, *because you and I are . . .*

Frog paused.

"*What?*" Charlie asked.

Frog hooked one index finger on top of the other one. Then she switched, and hooked the bottom index finger on top.

FRIENDS.

Charlie grinned—a grin so big his face hurt. That was one sign he wouldn't forget.

"*Friends,*" Charlie signed.

Frog nodded. "*That.*"

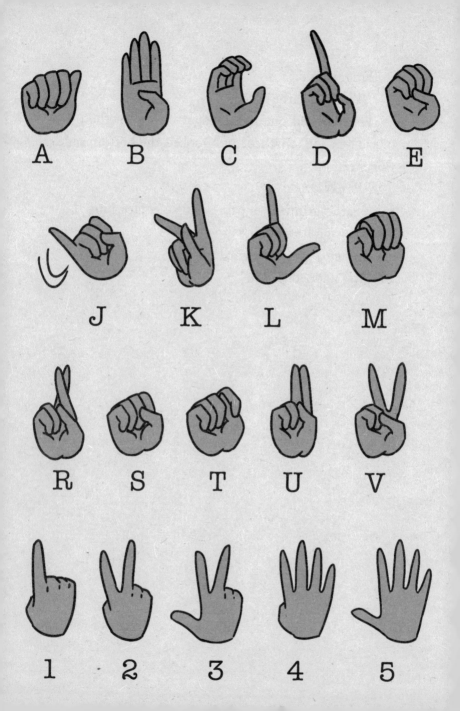

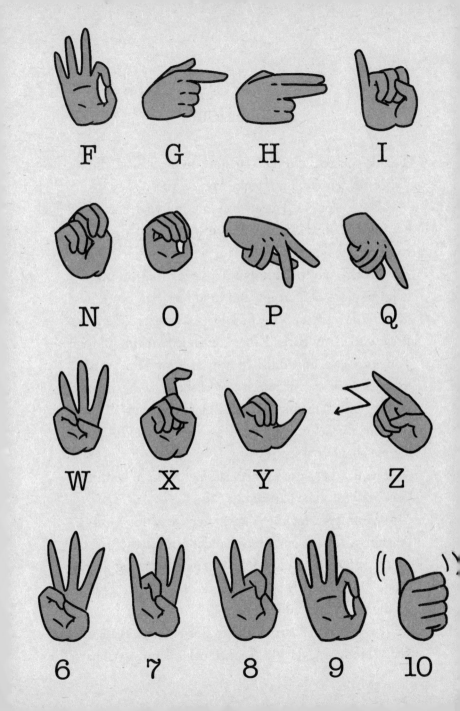

# Acknowledgments
## (Kiss-fist!)

Thank you to Jennifer Carlson, my agent and fellow Trixie Belden fan. I am lucky to have you!

Thank you to Tracey Keevan for your insightful editing. I learned so much working with you. Thank you to the entire team at Disney Hyperion.

Thank you to Vermont College of Fine Arts, a magical place of learning and kindness. Jane Kurtz was my first advisor at VCFA. I began writing *Charlie & Frog* with Amy Sarig King, continued writing it with Tom Birdseye, and finished a draft with Tim Wynne-Jones. I took transformative workshops with Amanda Jenkins and Martine Leavitt. Thank you my dearest advisors, for helping me grow as a writer, and for helping me shape this story.

Thank you to my VCFA classmates, the Inkredibles. I am grateful to be part of our class.

Thank you to the interpreters I work with in Washington, DC, and at Gallaudet University. You are a remarkable group of people who help me think deeply about "the work." A special thank-you to Kyle Duarte for the final copyedit reading.

Thank you to Derrick Behm, Joshua Josa, Bridgette Keefe-Hodgson, Jackie Lightfoot, Glenn Lockhart, and Diana Sea Markel. You six people were incredibly gracious to read *Charlie & Frog* and give me feedback, especially on the Deaf perspective. Your input was essential.

Thank you to Janis Cole, Allen Markel, Stephanie A. Sforza, and Steve Walker for suggestions regarding my ASL sign descriptions. Any errors are my own.

Thank you to Bill Gibson, from the District of Columbia Public Library, for answering my questions about the Dewey decimal system.

Thank you to my superfans—Glenn, Chris, Natalie, Patrick, and Shane Hulse. Every writer should have a Hulse and a Cape May front porch in her life. Thank you for being family.

Thank you to my heart-listeners: Karen Levy Newnam, Linda Johnson, Karen Schachter, Heidi Bachman, Andrea Pokorny, Ann Ewell, Lucille Mulich, Dolly Thomas, Monica Mulich, Kris Jaeckle, Diana O'Toole, Amy King Martellock, Ellen Petterson, Mary Ann Warner, Lynne Riedesel, Gwen Rubinstein, Selma Patillo-Simms, Liz Stone, Susan Botkin, K. J. Hagen, Beth Steinberg, and Betty Colonomos, founder of the life-changing Etna Project.

Thank you to the Schiefen, Ackroyd, More, Flick, Della Pesca, Newnam, and Levy families—for your love and support.

Thank you to my VCFA "best roommate ever!" Beth

Bacon. Thank you for reading this manuscript—the second time in the eleventh hour, giving me invaluable feedback both times. I am so grateful we experienced VCFA together.

Thank you to Helen Kemp Zax, for the amazing amount of time you gave this manuscript. *Charlie & Frog* benefited hugely from your input. I benefit hugely from your love and friendship.

Thank you to my mom, Louise Shults, for your creativity, for loving me, and being so proud of me. Paul, thank you for loving my mom.

Thank you to my dad, Billy More, Joe Cool jazz pianist, for the love you gave Kevin and me. I miss you so much.

Thank you to my daughters, Hayley and Isa. You both have been wonderful inspirations for my writing. Eugene, welcome to the family!

Thank you to my husband, David. I pushed you out of the way to get to the jelly doughnuts—and you still married me. You are a heart-listener extraordinaire. There is no one I admire more than you.

Finally, my everlasting gratitude goes to the Deaf community. Thank you for your resiliency, your determination, your beauty, your humor, your language, and your heart. Frog was easy to write because of you.

That.

Turn the page for a sneak peek!

# Charlie & FroG

# The Boney Hand

## A MYSTERY

# 1. Cute

Myra and Alistair Tickler were trying not to be lousy parents. Really, they were. They were even reading books—parenting books—from the Castle-on-the-Hudson library. One book recommended something called quality time, which Mr. and Mrs. Tickler were spending right now with Charlie, who was wedged between them on the couch, as everyone waited for the commercials to be over and for *Vince Vinelli's Worst Criminals Ever!* to come back on.

Everyone except for Grandma and Grandpa Tickler. They loved the commercials.

"Oh, it's the cow that wears purple glasses commercial!" said Grandma Tickler from her E-Z chair recliner. "I love the cow with purple glasses!"

Grandma Tickler held a jar of jellybeans on her lap, eating them one by one. Whenever she found a black jellybean, she gave it to Grandpa Tickler.

"Ayuh," said Grandpa Tickler from his own E-Z chair recliner.

"That's true, Irving," said Grandma Tickler. "The cow really does see better with purple glasses."

Most of the time Grandpa Tickler spoke one word: "ayuh." "Ayuh" meant "yes," but for Grandpa Tickler it also could mean a thousand other things. Luckily Grandma Tickler understood nine hundred and ninety-nine of them.

As for Charlie, he was trying to rehearse for tomorrow.

He had to do well tomorrow.

He didn't want to think about what would happen if he didn't do well tomorrow.

But it was hard to move his arms and practice his sign language with his parents sitting so quality-time close to him. Plus the criminals, their crimes, and the commercials were at full volume (even though the closed captions were on), making it hard for Charlie to concentrate.

"Vince Vinelli," Mrs. Tickler remarked during the

cow commercial, "seems like a very violent show to be watching during our quality time with Charlie. Don't you agree, Alistair?"

"Indeed I do, Myra," said Mr. Tickler. He held up the current book he was reading: *How to be a Great Parent in Only Seven Days!*

"This book clearly states that violent shows are not good for children. Or adults," added Mr. Tickler. He wrote himself a note in his parenting notebook. He and Mrs. Tickler were learning how to be good parents to Charlie, and that meant lots of reading and note-taking.

Normally Charlie would have agreed with his parents—violent shows are not good for children.

But Charlie *had* to watch Vince Vinelli.

And there were lots of shows to watch, for in addition to the regular Friday night program, there were *Vince Vinelli Special Edition!* episodes as well.

When Vince Vinelli came back on, he leaned into the camera with a serious look.

"Viewers, I want to take a short break from our worst criminals to ask you an important question." Vince looked off in the distance as if gathering his thoughts. Then he nodded and returned his gaze to the camera.

"Have you ever," Vince asked, "wanted to be a detective but didn't know how to start?"

"Yes!" said Grandma Tickler.

"Ayuh!" said Grandpa Tickler.

"Well, stop wanting right now," Vince told them. "Because for only $9.99 you can buy Vince Vinelli's When Crime Is a Fact, Good People Act detective kit. Inside this box is everything two people will need to look like real detectives—for only $9.99!"

"$9.99? That's a bargain!" Grandma Tickler said. She put down the jellybeans, reached for the pencil and newspaper on the table next to her, and wrote down the phone number flashing on the screen.

"But, Grandma," Charlie said, "it's $9.99 a month for *twelve months*. See the tiny words under the flashing numbers?"

Charlie stopped practicing long enough to do the math in his head. *Turn the 9.99 into a ten, and then multiply the ten by twelve. . . .*

"That's almost one hundred and twenty dollars," Charlie said.

"And if you order right now," Vince Vinelli continued, "I'll throw in a Vince Vinelli's Good People Do Good Things certificate absolutely free!"

"Not absolutely free," Charlie said, "because you still have to pay $9.99 a month for twelve months."

But Grandma Tickler wasn't listening. Grandma Tickler loved to buy things advertised on television.

"Yvette!" Grandma Tickler yelled for their house-keeper. "Where's my purse? Irving, we have to order that kit right now or we won't get the good people certificate. And we're good people!"

"Stop shouting, Irma," said Yvette as she came into the living room. "It's right here."

"You can't buy that, Mother," Mr. Tickler protested. "It's a waste of money!"

"But it's their money," Yvette said. "They can buy what they like—as silly as it might be."

"It's not silly!" said Grandma Tickler. "We need those detective outfits! How else are we going to fight crime?"

"You're not," Yvette said. "Just because someone looks like a detective doesn't make them a detective."

But once again Grandma Tickler wasn't listening. She reached for the phone next to her E-Z chair recliner as another commercial came on.

Yvette sat down in the rocking chair next to the couch.

"Has he read one yet?" Yvette asked Charlie.

"After these commercials," Charlie said. "I hope."

When Vince Vinelli had announced that he would be reading fan letters at the end of each show, his best friend, Frog, immediately began writing him a letter every day. Frog not only told Vince how much she loved his show, she told him all about herself. Frog told him her dream was to become a detective. Frog couldn't, of course, tell Vince Vinelli that she already was a detective since she and Charlie had solved their first mystery—she had to keep that a secret.

Charlie supposed that Vince Vinelli must get thousands of letters, but he still watched every episode, hoping Vince would read one of the letters Frog had sent. Charlie knew how much it would mean to her.

He tried to continue practicing his sign language. Charlie could see what he needed to do in his head. He just hoped his head would tell his hands what to do when the time came.

What would happen if his head forgot?

After the commercials about a skateboarding cat and a medicine that would help your headache but possibly paralyze you, *Vince Vinelli's Worst Criminals Ever!* came back on.

"It's now time," Vince said, "for that special part of my show that viewers have come to love—Vince Vinelli Fan Letter Time!"

Charlie stopped practicing. "This is it!" Charlie said. "Fingers crossed!"

Charlie, Yvette, and Grandpa Tickler crossed their fingers. They always crossed their fingers at this part of the show. Even Grandma Tickler, who was waiting to place her order, crossed her fingers on one hand while holding the phone with the other.

"Why are we crossing our fingers?" asked Mrs. Tickler.

"For Frog," Charlie said.

"Who's Frog?" asked Mr. Tickler.

"His best friend," snapped Yvette.

Charlie's parents dutifully crossed their fingers, too.

"I love it when my fans write to me," Vince was saying. "Of course, I mostly love it when they write *about* me." Vince chuckled but quickly grew serious again. "Sometimes, though, my fans write about themselves. It's important that I read those letters too, especially when the letters are from kids—"

Charlie squeezed his crossed fingers tighter.

"—because kids have dreams, just like adults do!"

In his mind Charlie signed "*dream.*" Ever since he had started school at the Castle School for the Deaf, Charlie thought about sign language all the time.

"And kids with dreams," Vince Vinelli continued, "have been writing me letters—"

Charlie held his breath.

"—such as this little girl who wrote me a letter—"

Charlie squeezed every single part of his body as tightly as he could.

"—a little girl named—"

Say it, Charlie thought. Say Frog's name.

"—Francine Castle!"

"FROG!" Charlie, Yvette, and Grandma Tickler screamed at the same time.

"AYUH!" Grandpa Tickler yelled.

Charlie and Yvette jumped up and down. Grandma Tickler waved the phone receiver around. Grandpa Tickler pumped a fist in the air. Mr. and Mrs. Tickler, unsure of what was happening, politely clapped.

Vince Vinelli held up Frog's letter, written on her favorite frog stationery, in his very tan hands.

"Yes, viewers," Vince continued, "little Francine Castle, also known as Frog, wrote me a letter. Little Froggy told me her dream is to become a detective!"

Why did Vince Vinelli keep calling Frog "little?" Charlie wondered. And why was he calling her Froggy? Nobody called her Froggy.

Vince looked deeply into the camera. "Little girl, little Froggy, keep your little dream alive—"

Charlie desperately wished Vince Vinelli would stop saying the words "little" and "Froggy."

"—because," Vince said, "maybe, just maybe, you will become a detective someday. But if you order Vince Vinelli's When Crime Is a Fact, Good People Act detective kit"—Vince flashed his blinding smile—"then you definitely will!"

The camera panned to Vince Vinelli's When Crime Is a Fact, Good People Act detective kit, sitting next to Vince in its bright red box. Vince gave the box a little pat, and then looked deeply into the camera.

"Viewers, little Froggy told me she is deaf and

communicates in American Sign Language. So for little deaf Froggy I learned one sign—one special sign that describes her."

Please, Charlie silently begged, let the sign be "*powerful*" or "*amazing*."

Vince touched his index and middle fingers to his chin, thumb extended, and then swiped them downward twice. "*Cute!*" Vince Vinelli signed and then spoke.

"How nice!" said Mrs. Tickler.

"Very!" said Mr. Tickler.

"No," Charlie groaned.

"Because," Vince Vinelli said, "that's what this fan letter is, and that's what you are little Froggy—"

"Stop," Charlie said.

"—very, very—"

"Don't," Charlie said.

"—*cute!*" Vince Vinelli signed it once more.

"So sweet!" said Mrs. Tickler.

"And such an honor," said Mr. Tickler. "Vince Vinelli is very famous, you know."

Grandma Tickler covered the phone with her hand. "Frog isn't cute, is she, Irving?"

"Ayuh," said Grandpa Tickler.

"I didn't think so," said Grandma Tickler.

"You know what Frog is?" Yvette said. "Frog is furious right now, that's what Frog is."

Charlie agreed. But at least, Charlie told himself,

Frog couldn't hear Vince Vinelli's tone of voice. But just then the person typing the closed captions had felt compelled to add one more sentence:

(*Vince Vinelli is speaking in a voice that adults use to talk to very little children.*)

Charlie sighed. Frog was definitely furious.